ADVENTURES OF A
VEGAN VAMP

CATE LAWLEY

ALSO BY CATE LAWLEY

VEGAN VAMP

Adventures of a Vegan Vamp

The Client's Conundrum

The Elvis Enigma

The Nefarious Necklace

DEATH RETIRED

Death Retires

THE GOODE WITCH MATCHMAKER

Timely Love

Ghostly Love

Deathly Love

Forgotten Love

The Goode Witch Matchmaker Collection

Writing as Kate Baray

LOST LIBRARY

Lost Library

Spirited Legacy

Defensive Magic

Lost Library Collection: Books 1-3

Witch's Diary

Lost Library Shorts Collection

The Covered Mirror: A Lost Library Halloween Short

Krampus Gone Wild: A Lost Library Christmas Short

SPIRELLI PARANORMAL INVESTIGATIONS

Spirelli Paranormal Investigations Season 1

Entombed: A Spirelli Investigations Novel

Writing as K.D. Baray

BEAUREGARD

Mistaken: A Seth Beauregard Short

For CS and EOC. You've made writing a reality rather than a possibility.

BONUS CONTENT

Interested in bonus content for the Vegan Vamp series?
Subscribe to my newsletter to receive a bonus chapter for
Adventures of a Vegan Vamp as well as release
announcements and other goodies! Sign up at
http://eepurl.com/b6pNQP.

PROLOGUE

I died a little. I wish I could say it was a blur, but it's a blank. A mystery. I was an anxiety-ridden, overachieving, successful (and perhaps not entirely likable) professional—and human. I definitely started this story very human. But now I'm none of those things.

This story is about the murder of that woman and catching the man who killed her. It's also about how I became a vampire and also a little about how becoming a vampire was the best thing that could have happened to me.

1

THE NIGHT I DIED A LITTLE

"Mallory, darling, you're buying tonight, aren't you?" Liz, with her sleek red hair, high cheekbones, and long legs made my skin itch with jealous annoyance.

How could she even walk in those impossible heels?

"Sure." I knew she'd ditch her usual drink for a premium, but that was Liz.

Actually, that was the entire work gang: Liz, Shelley, Martin, and Penelope. They invited me when they wanted free drinks, because I picked up the tab when I tagged along. At least, that was my suspicion. I made more money than the rest of them, and they knew it. That created tension.

How was it my fault they couldn't negotiate their salary better?

I handed the bartender my debit card and pointed to the fearsome foursome to my right, indicating I'd be paying for their round.

The guy was kind of cute in a tight-T-shirt, skinny-jeans, bearded-hipster way, but he didn't make eye contact. He grabbed my card, swiped it to open my tab, and handed it back to me.

Cute bartender guy didn't even look up when I gave him my drink order: a white wine spritzer. I might not be five foot nine with killer cheekbones and a glamorous sense of style, but not all of his patrons could look like Liz.

At least he was fast. My drink arrived—after Liz's, Shelley's, Martin's, and Penelope's—but still pretty quickly. I tried not to sigh. My suit was expensive and well-tailored, my makeup reasonably fresh, and I was having a good hair day. And—the most important factor—*I was picking up the tab.*

So what was it that made people like the hipster bartender slip right over me as if I didn't exist?

Or like I smelled really bad? I discreetly sniffed. No. My supercharged twenty-four-hour antiperspirant was doing its job.

He was just a jerk with a brain that worked significantly less than his biceps—or some other part of his anatomy.

Liz turned to include me in the conversation, so I inched closer. It had to be work related.

Penelope had a self-satisfied smirk on her face. "I was just saying, our new boss plans to fire two people from our division. I heard from a *very* reliable source. And you know how much they like to clean out inflated salaries whenever the opportunity arises."

My lips curved slightly. "Or those with the lowest performance evaluations."

Penelope's nostrils flared. The spiteful heat of her stare bounced off me with no effect. Again, not my fault that she spent as much time on social media as she did doing client work.

"Still, when looking at tightening up the budget, it

makes sense that bloated salaries would be targeted." Martin looked at me with a certain glee that made him appear, just for a moment, as vicious as he actually was.

Martin was not someone I envisioned as having a mother. Hatched, maybe, but not born.

A half-swallowed chuckle almost gagged me, but I managed to keep white wine spritzer from spurting out my nose—barely. The image of Martin emerging fully formed, more reptile than mammal, from the remains of an eggshell was impossible to erase. I tried not to snigger.

He was such a loathsome being that I couldn't help but cling to that image as my own private revenge. I would never forget the opportunities he'd stolen from me, the rumors he'd spread, the trouble he'd stirred up with clients. I'd overcome the obstacles he'd thrown in my path, time after time, but he'd made my life—my success at work—much more difficult.

Martin glared, as if he could see the image I'd conjured. "Really, Mallory. No one will be surprised if they fire you. Your interpersonal skills are somewhat lacking—as I'm sure more than one supervisor has told you. You're not popular with the clients."

Which wasn't exactly true. I was quite good at my job, and I may not always make the best first impression—helped along by a quietly whispered word or two by Martin —but when it came down to getting work done well, my clients knew I was reliable. And organized. Efficient, over-achieving, hardworking... I was all of those things.

Perhaps that explained why my coworkers never accepted me. Why I was always on the outside looking in. I was substantially better at my job, and that made me less likable. At least I was self-aware enough to realize it. Changing it? That was simply a step too far. I am what I am.

I understood all of this, but why they additionally felt the need to blame me for their failings, that was a puzzle.

How Penelope's Facebook addiction, Liz's penchant for sleeping with married coworkers, and Martin's general sliminess—all factors that had impeded their careers—were any fault of mine, I would never understand.

My eyes passed over Shelley. At least Shelley was okay. She'd never been blatantly spiteful like the others in my division, but she was hardly warm.

I closed my eyes and imagined I was at home in my apartment. A restful space away from these people. It was exhausting being the person everyone blamed and no one liked.

Why do it? I didn't need the hassle. Fitting in wasn't worth it—especially when there was zero chance I'd ever actually be accepted. When I opened my eyes, a second wine spritzer was in front of me. I tried to catch the bartender's gaze to thank him, but he'd already moved on to a blonde, beautiful customer.

I drained my first drink and quickly started in on the second. As soon as I finished it, I was headed home. And I was done with these little after work gatherings for good.

Thankfully, my apartment was within walking distance, so I could chug that spritzer with a clear conscience.

2

THE FLU

W hy did my mouth feel like it had been stuffed with cotton balls? I tried to swallow and almost threw up in my mouth.

Not good. Very not good. I held my breath and fought the urge to swallow again.

I needed to be absolutely still. Moving made me want to ralph, and I would never make it to the bathroom.

Even the thought of moving made my head pound with a vicious rhythm.

My eyelid cracked of its own volition and the pain at the base of my skull and behind my eyes ratcheted up. I carefully shut my eyes and lay very, very still.

Finally, after counting backward from a hundred, I started to feel myself drift away.

❧

A DESERT SURROUNDED ME. A cool desert. A cool, dry desert.

Slowly, I became aware of the feel of the sheets against

my skin, the pillow under my head. And then the parched, cottony feel of my mouth.

I almost groaned—almost—but then I remembered the gut-piercing, brain-pounding pain from earlier. The feeling that my head would explode into a billion tiny pieces. So I didn't make a sound.

Time passed. A little? A lot? I lay in my bed—still, in pain, and afraid—for I don't know how long...but then I realized I was thirsty. Wandering-the-desert, no-water-for-days thirsty.

I opened my mouth a little and experimented with moving my lips. The pulling sensation that forewarned of cracking skin stopped me.

Water had *never* sounded so glorious. I could feel it slipping past my lips, moistening my mouth... And then I did groan, because there was no water.

And my head exploded in pain, followed by a black nothingness.

SOMEONE HAD SUPERGLUED my eyelids shut. Somewhere in the back of my brain, I realized that was B.A.D. Kidnapping, home invasion, a *Criminal Minds*-type serial killer—scenarios flashed through my mind.

But I wasn't afraid. I experienced, in fact, a complete absence of fear. I was simply too tired to feel any strong emotion.

I must have drifted off to sleep again, because when I woke up I vaguely remembered thoughts of superglue and kidnapping, but this time I realized how insane that was, mostly because I could open my eyes—just.

It took some delicate prying, but I managed to eventually see the light of day. I'd had allergy attacks that left my eyes crunchy—I lived in allergy central, a.k.a. Austin, Texas —but the crud in my eyes was something entirely different.

Whatever the funky goo was, the effort of unsticking my eyelashes from it had wiped me out. I lay on my bed and tried to summon up sufficient energy to move, but it wasn't happening.

Lying there with my mind awake and my body incapacitated, I couldn't help but dwell on my drier-than-dirt mouth. I tried to lick my lips, but it didn't help.

I needed a drink. *Water.* I almost shivered, I was so excited. The thought of water was finally enough to make me think about getting up.

At least the gnarly headache that I'd been sporting the last time I woke up was gone. But I had crystal-clear memories of that pain, and it was those memories that made me cautious. I slowly rolled onto my side. My muscles protested. The deep muscle aches made me wonder if I'd come down with the flu.

Headache, nausea, aching muscles—I stopped inventorying my symptoms and lifted the back of my hand to my forehead and then my cheek. Dry and cool to the touch; no fever. A feverless flu? I also had the oddest feeling that I hadn't moved since I'd fallen asleep. And I *never* slept on my back; I was a side sleeper.

Flu or no flu, that water wasn't getting any closer. In one quick motion, I rolled off my bed and onto my feet—and promptly collapsed in a heap on the floor.

Abstract thoughts of superglued eyes and kidnapping hadn't done it, but now I was worried. I needed a drink. How long had I been asleep? And I still didn't feel like I needed to pee. I *always* had to pee as soon as I woke up. I had to be dangerously dehydrated.

Where was my phone? I usually left it plugged in next to my bed, and it was hard to believe I'd slept through my alarm. Mustering up enough energy to crawl, I inched my way to the bedside table where my phone was plugged in. With what seemed a monumental effort, I grabbed the phone. I propped myself up against my bed and tapped the screen.

Nuts. Fourteen missed calls, twenty texts...how...? It was late and I'd missed work, but fourteen missed calls. A nasty feeling washed over me. The wallpaper on my phone had a large digital clock that read nine fifty-three—but there was no date. I flicked the screen down. My eyes didn't want to focus. Or my mind was playing tricks. Friday the twentieth. That simply wasn't possible; I'd gone for happy hour drinks on Tuesday. I couldn't have been in bed for three days. Someone would have checked on me...wouldn't they?

After dialing voicemail, I tapped the speaker button and then started to scroll through my texts. After five minutes it was clear: no one had thought to check on me. I'd been berated for not calling in, for missing appointments, and for failing to attend meetings. By my boss and my coworkers. By voicemail and text. I'd made a mistake, and they'd reveled in it.

The effort of retrieving my phone had so depleted my strength that I couldn't do more than lie on the floor. So I curled up and wallowed in self-pity.

To be so alone that no one suspected I was unwell or injured after I'd been missing for three days? Miserable. Pathetic. A desolate existence. I realized as I cried that no tears fell.

I hacked out dry sobs that burned my throat, because I'd never made it to the bathroom for that drink of water.

3

HOW AM I ALIVE?

I was broken.

Something was wrong with me, with my body, and I had two days to find out what it was. Two days, and even then I'd probably be begging to keep my job, if those texts and voicemails were any indication. I needed to sort out what was happening to me, and I also needed some kind of believable excuse explaining away my three days off the grid.

Last night I'd eventually managed to make it to the bathroom, consume an unbelievable quantity of water, and fall asleep again. Here it was, ten a.m. on Saturday, and I still hadn't peed. What person goes four days without peeing?

After trawling the internet, I discovered people did go four days and even longer without urinating, but none of the scenarios I'd found seemed likely to apply to me. Thank you, Google.

Going to the doctor seemed wise, imperative even... except for the part where I had to get out of bed, get dressed, and actually get there. I rolled over in bed. Then I rolled again and sat up. The soreness was gone. I was exhausted, yes, but the deep muscle aches had vanished.

Tired I could manage. I'd pulled a few all-nighters in business school and knew some tricks. Group projects still left a nasty taste in my mouth. There was always one under-achiever who didn't do their part, and never in a predictable, manageable way. Experience taught me that I could push through exhaustion with determination (which I had in spades), caffeine (which waited in the kitchen), and a shower (which sounded delightful).

After I'd put the kettle on to boil and ground some fresh beans, I sat down with my laptop at the kitchen table. I drafted a quick note to my boss that I'd come down with a terrible flu, hadn't left my bed in days, and would be back to work on Monday. I groveled as best I could, reread it to make sure I sounded sincerely apologetic without tumbling into desperation, and then clicked send.

It all sounded reasonable enough but for one small detail: my boss had actually met me. Anyone that had spent more than a few minutes with me would know that I'd call in in between puking bouts. The only thing that could keep me from calling in was a coma. Or death. The piercing whistle of the kettle distracted me from pursuing that morbid thought.

Five minutes later, I marched into my bathroom with my French-pressed coffee in hand, ready to tick off the next item on my list. A shower should be a nice pick-me-up. Although—oddly enough—I didn't feel like I'd spent the last four days sick in bed. And I hadn't noticed any weird odors.

If you didn't shower for four days, you smelled. A simple fact of life every woman past puberty understands. But what would I tell my doctor? I'm fresh as a daisy even when I don't shower—isn't that weird? I shook my head and turned to flip the water on.

Hot coffee splashed my thighs as my mug fell from nerveless fingers, and the sound of shattering ceramic echoed in my ears as if from a great distance.

The gaunt-faced image across from me jumped, and I yelped in surprise.

Her mouth moved as if yelping in surprise.

I took a cautious step away from her...and she did the same in reverse.

"Oh, no. Nononono." I lifted my hand to my shockingly thin face. "No."

My knees ceased supporting my weight, and I sank down to perch on the lip of the tub. And for the first time since I'd gained consciousness the previous evening, I looked closely at my hands. Long, elegant fingers. Too thin to be my fingers. I inspected my right hand and found no age spot just below the knuckle of my index finger. No blemishes at all. The fine lines that had become invisible to me over the last few years were marked now by their absence.

My forearms had become a series of interconnected freckles more years ago than I could remember. Since my mid-twenties, maybe? A light, even tan now covered my forearms.

I dropped my head into my hands, but that was a mistake. My own flesh felt alien. My face had once had a pleasant roundness to it that I'd become accustomed to. The new sharpness of my chin and the definition of my cheekbones felt foreign under my fingertips.

Inhale, two, three. Exhale, two, three. Inhale, two, three. Exhale, two, three.

That therapist had been good for something after all, because when I opened my eyes I had a plan. I stood up and stripped off all of my clothes. I was taking a shower, because that had been the plan before I'd found some alien person's body had replaced my own.

I tried not to think too much as I scrubbed myself down in the shower. I was about to wash my hair when I realized that it was clean. I usually had to shampoo daily. "Not thinking, Mallory. Just showering." And I rinsed my hair really well without shampooing it. On a whim, I went ahead and conditioned it so I'd have the perfumed illusion of having washed my hair.

When I stepped out of the shower and wrapped myself in a towel, I found the hem, as always, just above my knee, but my towel wrapped much further around than it should. Without pausing to acknowledge the gaunt, dark-headed woman in the mirror, I left the bathroom for my walk-in closet.

Smacking the light switch on gave me an odd sense of satisfaction. Maybe if I slammed a door, I'd feel even better. I steeled myself, then let the towel drop. Turning to the full-length mirror, I tried to examine the woman standing there dispassionately. The eyes were mine. So much larger in my now too-thin face, but the shape, color, and the thick lashes were all me. A glimmer of hope pushed past the panic. I was still in there. The shape of my face had changed significantly, but the flare of my eyebrows was the same, as was the shape of my nose. As I tilted my head to the side, I realized it was really my jaw line that had changed the most.

My gaze slipped lower to prominent collarbones and—

"No way." I could see my ribs, barely, but I could see them. And my D cups had diminished to a less voluptuous A or B. I wasn't sure which, because I couldn't remember having ever been an A or B. I had starved, literally, in four days. No one lost that much body mass that fast.

That's why I was so tired. And also why my brain had ceased to function properly. If I hadn't eaten in four days, of course I was tired. And my blood sugar was low. I threw on some yoga pants and a T-shirt—nothing else would fit—and hopped on the scales in my bathroom. I'd lost twenty-five pounds. How was that possible?

I stepped away from the scales and tried to decide if I was actually hungry. I wasn't. What was happening to me? I didn't even know what I would tell my doctor. He was a stuffy old guy who barely spoke ten words to me during any visit. He'd think I'd starved myself, but I would never. I *liked* food. And while I'd been a little overweight, I didn't have a serious problem with the way I looked before. Sure, I envied more glamorous women—who didn't? I squeezed my eyes shut. Looking so different, feeling so alien in my own body, I missed being a little overweight, because that was *me.*

Food—that was my next step. I needed to eat something.

En route to the kitchen, I contemplated my two biggest dilemmas: what story could I tell my coworkers to explain my rapid weight loss? And how could I convince my doctor I hadn't developed an eating disorder?

If I couldn't sell my doc on the fact that I hadn't suddenly stopped eating, then he wouldn't bother to figure out what was wrong with me. And as I realized the truth of that conclusion, I also realized how insane it was that he was still my GP. Why was I still seeing that clown? It was past time to find a new doctor who might actually listen and perhaps believe me when I said I wasn't starving myself.

A knock on the front door startled me. Once I'd recovered from the shock of the unexpected noise, I detoured from the kitchen to the front door. I was even a little bit happy to have a temporary distraction from the craziness of my dilemma.

But then I opened the door to a shocked neighbor, and it occurred to me (belatedly) that interacting with people who knew me as twenty-five pounds heavier might not be advisable.

"Hi, Mrs. A. How have you been?"

"My, but you certainly look different, don't you, Mallory? Have you been ill? Not that you look, uh... You look just fine." She pursed her lips together.

I scrambled to think of an excuse, any excuse, for my appearance. "Diet pills from Mexico..." I shrugged, leaving the rest to her imagination.

"I see." She frowned, clearly disapproving of such newfangled methods. She'd told me not long after I moved in that she enjoyed a brisk walk twice daily and ate salad for dinner every night. From the context of the conversation, it had been a not-so-subtle hint that I should consider doing the same. Mrs. A's face cleared, and she leaned forward. "Well, it's just that I've been knocking and knocking. I didn't want to use my key, just in case...in case you might have *company*." She whispered the last word like it was a secret she was hiding from nosy neighbors. Except she was the only nosy neighbor on this side of the fourth floor.

I stood up straighter and bit my lip in an effort not to laugh. Once I let the hysteria take hold, it might not let go.

Mrs. A was embarrassed that her thirty-nine-year-old neighbor might have had male company overnight. The absurdity of it all was too much. I'd been dying—literally wasting away in my apartment—and the only neighbor with a key was too embarrassed by my (wholly imagined) sexual marathon to use her key.

Biting back a laugh that was sure to be wildly misinterpreted, I said, "No, I haven't had any company. Just a little flu bug. Thank you for checking on me."

She gave me a sweet, grandmotherly smile, but she had a wicked glint in her eye—like she knew the *real* story. "I see. Well, if I'd known you were sick, I'd have brought over some homemade chicken soup for you."

Mrs. A had a vivid imagination, and she did love to spy on the neighbors—but envisioning an orgy in my apartment was a level beyond anything I would have previously expected of her. She needed to get out more. I smiled and tried to look thankful—even though I'd tried her chicken soup. "That's so kind of you, but I'm on the mend now."

I took a step back deeper into my apartment, hoping she'd get the hint.

Mrs. A was no one's fool. "You let me know if you change your mind about that soup. Bye for now." She gave me a jaunty wave and headed back to her apartment just across the hall.

As I closed the door, I gauged my level of hunger. All that talk of chicken soup should have sparked a little twinge of hunger—but no. Time to try a little food and see if that perked up my appetite. Sometimes all it took was that first bite, and then, poof, my stomach was jumpstarted. Not that I'd gone quite this long without a meal, but in my school days, I'd definitely skipped a few.

As I wandered into the kitchen, I considered my current mental state after four days with no food. How I wasn't light-headed and seeing stars, I had no clue.

Nothing in the pantry looked particularly appealing. The refrigerator had been practically empty before I'd fallen ill, so I wasn't holding out much hope there. Orange juice looked good—probably because my mouth still had a cottony, dry feeling. I drank straight from the carton as I perused the rest of the contents. Sandwich meat that had been opened longer than seven days, bread for toast, a questionable tomato, and more condiments than any three people needed.

Eventually I settled on peanut butter toast. Easy, filling, and about all my bare cupboards were going to yield.

It wasn't until I loaded my toaster oven that the oddness of drinking straight from the carton hit me. Normally, I found that disgusting: backwash in the carton, the juice sitting in the fridge, and the bacteria from my mouth growing and overpopulating the previously pristine orange juice... I blinked. My scalp wasn't crawling. I had no urge to immediately chuck the OJ into the trash or brush my teeth. Bizarre.

Not that I was OCD. I was just particular. And I didn't like bacteria and germs. Or bugs. Or sick people. My hand was moving toward the carton of OJ for another sip when the timer on the toaster oven dinged.

Apparently I was thirsty enough not to care about bacteria, because that OJ sounded really good. I shrugged and chugged the rest of the juice.

The peanut butter melted as I spread it on the warm toast, and the nutty aroma filled the room. My mouth watered. I took a bite, and as the gooey peanut butter hit my tongue, I experienced my first pangs of hunger.

I savored the warmth of the peanut butter and the crunch of the crust. It was heavenly.

A strange sensation was the first indication that all was not well. Nothing I could pinpoint, just a notion that something wasn't quite right. If only that feeling had persisted for more than a few seconds, I might have realized what it meant. The contents of my stomach were spread on the floor before I could even think about making it to the bathroom.

Tiptoeing around the mess, I made a dash for the sink. I

rinsed my mouth as best I could, but when the acrid taste in my mouth was finally gone, I didn't know what to do. Was it the orange juice? The bread? The peanut butter?

I had managed to keep down the water I'd drunk so far, but that was all I knew for sure.

As I rinsed my mouth a second time, I realized I still had no good story for my doctor and a nasty mess to clean up. Trawling the Internet for a new doctor just moved up my to-do list. I had to sort myself out, and preferably before Monday. My job was my life—so technically, my life was on the line.

And then there was the question of how much longer I could go without food. Maybe there was more to my life than my job. Was my actual physical well-being in jeopardy? But that couldn't be. I didn't feel *that* bad.

I threw a mountain of towels on the floor so that there was no way I'd be contaminated by orange juice/peanut butter puke, and then chucked them all in the wash. Germs and bacteria may be less freaky today, but puke was still disgusting.

As soon as all traces of mess had been erased, I realized my short bout of activity had drained whatever energy reserves I had. I filled a pitcher with water and grabbed a cup to set on my bedside table, and then I followed the very inviting call of my bed.

4

NEW DOCTOR, NOT WITCHDOCTOR

M y eyelids popped open. I did a quick check for eyelid gunk, but my eyes were surprisingly clear of superglue funk. A buzzing energy filled me, not unlike a massive caffeine high. Not traditionally a morning person, that was more than a little surprising.

All of that energy was accompanied by a massive thirst that reminded me of the pitcher I'd filled earlier. I turned to my bedside table, planning to drain the pitcher—but it was already empty. Odd. I didn't remember waking up, and certainly didn't remember drinking an entire pitcher of water.

I made my way to the kitchen in search of liquids. I even considered braving some milk. But sanity returned when I remembered my earlier puke-fest. Water for now. After drinking three tall glasses, I filled a fourth glass and sat down at my computer. I needed to go to the doctor, preferably right now, while I still had the energy to get dressed and leave the house. Who knew how long that would last? And I needed a new doctor. My guy wasn't going to cut it. He didn't have weekend hours—and he just wasn't going to work.

Three rejections later, I'd exhausted the only options that fit my needs. Finding anyone with weekend hours, who was accepting new patients, and took my insurance, was apparently an impossible task. I tried to take a drink, but found I'd drained yet another glass of water. I stared at the empty glass. That was not normal.

I tried not to get frustrated, but I was on the clock. Who knew when my little energy boost would fade away, and I'd end up passed out in bed again for several hours?

With renewed determination, I scratched insurance off my list of requirements and kept searching. Five minutes later, I'd found a doctor who shared a clinic with several alternative medicine practitioners. Not sure how I felt about that, but she had weekend hours and the website declared, "New patients welcome." I wasn't holding my breath, because two other traditional doctors had said the same— but that didn't include new patients to be seen this weekend.

Also, I wasn't entirely sure what alternative medicine meant in the context of this practice. The two doctors on staff were both MDs, but it looked like the practice offered some other therapies. Maybe that meant they'd be open-minded about my weird symptoms? Or at least not assume I was starving myself intentionally. The thought was enough for me to dial the number.

"Doctor's office. How may I help you?" The chirpy voice on the line sounded helpful enough.

"I'm in urgent need of an appointment this weekend. Do you have any available?"

"Are you already a patient with us?"

I wanted to groan in frustration, but managed to filter

out my annoyance—I hoped. "No, but I really do need to see someone quickly."

"Well..." The young woman on the phone at least pretended that she wanted to help. So far, that was much better than the other calls.

I tried for a little pity. "My symptoms have been rather alarming, and I don't think an ER visit is going to be any help."

A loud sigh puffed across the line. "Tell me what your symptoms are, and—no promises—maybe we can fit you in on Monday or Tuesday."

That was the best offer I'd had so far.

"Rapid weight loss, persistent and unquenchable thirst, aching muscles—though that's gone now—and long periods of sleep. Oh—and I can't seem to keep food down." I reviewed my mental symptom checklist. "I think that's it."

"All right. I'll check in with the doctor, but she's quite busy today. We may not be back in touch until Monday. And if at any time you feel like there's an emergency, you should seek help from an urgent care facility or the emergency room."

"Yes, I understand that." I mentally shrugged as I gave her my contact details. Losing twenty-five pounds in days was likely a really big emergency—but I was mobile and staying hydrated. And I really, really didn't want to go to the ER. What would the ER do for me besides send me a massive bill? I was walking and talking and had no pain.

I was scrolling through alternative choices online, holding on to the ridiculous hope someone would see me before Monday, when my phone rang.

As I tapped accept, I realized it was the number for the alternative medicine clinic. "Hello?"

"This is Dr. Dobrescu. Is this Mallory Andrews?"

It hadn't even been five minutes, so the doctor obviously hadn't been *that* busy.

"Yes, that's me. Do you think you might get me in?"

"When did your symptoms start?" Brisk and businesslike, Dr. Dobrescu wasn't messing about.

"Maybe Tuesday? As I told your receptionist, I've been sleeping quite a bit, so I can't say exactly."

"Are you missing any time?"

"I'm not sure what—" I suddenly realized I had no idea how I got home from the bar. Two white wine spritzers wouldn't have that effect. "Ah, maybe."

Silence followed.

I checked to see that I hadn't accidentally ended the call, but it was still live on my end. "Dr. Dobrescu?"

"As soon as you can, come in."

"I'm sorry?"

"We'll fit you in. When can we expect you?"

The clinic had gone from "maybe Monday or Tuesday" to "come in now" in the space of minutes, and I hadn't even mentioned exactly how much weight I'd lost. I didn't think my symptoms were that specific—at least not according to Google. But given my situation, especially the part where I needed to show up at work on Monday to keep my job, I could hardly be choosy. "I can be there in forty-five minutes."

"We'll be ready for you."

I ended the call and then found myself staring at the phone. *We'll be ready for you.* The call had been just a little bit off. Or my imagination was running wild. Probably the latter given my less-than-stellar reasoning skills on an empty stomach.

Rooting around in my closet finally produced an old tennis skirt that almost fit and an only slightly oversized T-shirt. I skipped my usual shower, because I was on a tight timeline. I felt like a narcoleptic time bomb.

As I zipped along in my flashy red Audi TT, two things bothered me. I'd never thought my car was flashy before today, and I was less comfortable driving a new sports car than I was with the sad state of my attire. I couldn't remember the last time I'd been in public looking quite so rumpled. But the normal anxiety—that "what would people think" feeling that I normally suffered—simply wasn't there. It was liberating.

The office wasn't at all what I expected; it looked like any other doctor's office. The only thing different from my regular, cranky-old-man doctor's office was the speed with which the staff ushered me into an exam room. I typically waited fifteen to thirty minutes at a minimum. And it wasn't as if the practice wasn't busy. The receptionist hadn't exaggerated. I'd parked across the street because the office's lot had been full.

I sat down on the edge of the examining table and watched in surprise as the nurse or assistant—I wasn't sure which, because she hadn't bothered to introduce herself—disappeared out the door. She'd gone without taking a history, or commenting on when the doctor would be able to see me, or even a goodbye. Looking back, the only direct interaction I'd had with the staff was to confirm my name.

"Curiouser and curiouser." I flipped through the contacts in my phone, trying to find someone—anyone—that I could send a quick text with my location and a heads-up to check on me in an hour or so.

I didn't realize I'd spoken out loud until a woman's voice startled me with a reply. "Do you frequently feel like Alice?"

My eyes met the intent gaze of a dark-haired woman who carried a clipboard. Her delicate features and even skin tones made her age hard to determine, but I guessed anywhere between thirty and fifty. "Ah. No, actually. Just the last few days." I squinted to read her nametag: Dr. Dobrescu. "Don't you guys usually have your nurses take a history before you see patients?"

"There's some concern that you're contagious. If you don't mind, I'd like to eliminate that as a possibility before we proceed."

She still had that intent look, so I couldn't help wonder if there was a serious problem lurking. I'd stopped worrying quite so much, because—twenty-five pounds of rapid weight loss aside—I was feeling pretty good. My energy buzz hadn't faded yet. "How do you do that?"

"It's an in-house test. I just need to draw a little blood."

When I shrugged, she set her clipboard down and gloved up—twice.

"Don't you have a phlebotomist or a nurse or something for this stuff?"

"We're a small office." She approached with a metal tray.

Blatantly untrue, but I didn't think commenting would get me any answers. I watched her wrap a band around my upper arm and then swab a spot with alcohol, but after that I couldn't do it. Something about blood and needles always freaked me out—especially if it was a needle in *my* arm and *my* blood. I stared at a point on the wall, careful that I couldn't even catch what she was doing in my peripheral vision.

"You'll feel a small pinch now."

I choked on a laugh. Where did doctors learn that stuff? "Ow."

"Did that hurt?" She sounded genuinely surprised.

Really? She just shoved a needle in my arm, and she was surprised? What kind of doctor was this lady? Glancing in her direction and then quickly away when I caught sight of the tube filling with blood, I replied, "Well, it was more than a pinch."

"You said your symptoms began Tuesday?"

"I think so. That's the last time I remember being conscious."

"You can look now; I'm done."

"Also, I should mention that I've lost a lot of weight. I think maybe twenty-five pounds in the last few days. I can't be exactly sure because I hadn't weighed myself in a while, but close to that."

Still Dr. Dobrescu didn't meet my eyes. And she didn't seem surprised.

"Are you guys in touch with the CDC or something?"

Finally, I'd caught her attention. Dobrescu's head popped up from her clipboard. "What do you mean?"

She looked a little panicky.

"I just mean that you say I'm contagious, and my visit hasn't exactly been typical so far. You seem to know something about what's going on. Is there some kind of bug going around that you're on the lookout for?"

With a firm shake of her head, she said, "This will only take a moment." Finally, the woman gave me a close, intent look. Like she was peering into my soul. "Stay here."

Eyes wide, I replied as solemnly as I could, "I will."

Where the heck did she think I was going?

She wasn't gone that long, but when she came back she'd brought reinforcements. As in, a really large man who looked like he meant business. Tall, burly, and with a shaved head, I couldn't help thinking of the Mr. Clean commercials. Except Mr. Clean had a friendly, welcoming, I-want-to-clean-your-home vibe that this guy was lacking.

"Ah, is there some issue?" I scooted around on the end of

the exam table, trying to decide whether to hop off—and thereby trigger some reaction from the big guy—or to stay seated and wait for Dobrescu to sic her extra-large nurse on me. "You guys never even took a history or anything. Don't you want to know about my parents' health, whether I'm taking any medications, that type of thing?"

I didn't remember being this chatty when I was nervous...but maybe the chatter would distract them, and I wouldn't get tackled.

"We just need to make sure that you're safe before you leave." Dr. Dobrescu looked down at her clipboard. "How long ago did you first fall ill?"

The big guy blocked the door. And now that I looked past the shaved head, I noticed he wasn't wearing clogs—unlike the rest of the staff—and he wasn't wearing nurse scrubs. Hm. Not a nurse.

"Last Tuesday I was fine. I told you that before. So—what?—that was six days ago. You're a little bit freaking me out right now." And, of course, a little meant a lot. I glanced at the big guy.

She shared a look with the man then made a note. "Have you felt any violent urges?"

"Noooo."

Dr. Dobrescu looked up at me like she didn't buy it.

"You're making me very uncomfortable, and I'm considering my exit strategies. I'm all about the flight and not the fight."

Dr. Dobrescu scribbled furiously.

"Ah—you don't mean violence to myself, do you?"

The doctor's head bobbed up. "Have you been feeling a desire to self-harm? Or any suicidal thoughts?"

The woman looked much too excited about the prospect. I was starting to feel like a lab experiment.

"Not even a little. Are you going to tell me what's going on?"

She reached into her lab coat and pulled something out. She thrust it at me, and I grabbed it without thinking.

In my right hand, I held a tube filled with dark red...blood? "Ack!"

The vial fell from my fingers. It bounced off the edge of the exam table and then shattered on the floor. Bits of glass scattered, and blood seeped around the shards. "Nuts." I turned to the doctor with a nasty look. "Why would you do that? Couldn't you tell how much having my blood drawn freaked me out?"

The doctor had retreated to stand next to Mr. Clean near the door as I'd spoken.

Before I could worry much about the frantic scribbling and hushed whispers, my stomach rebelled. It started with a gentle roiling sensation when the odor of the blood first hit me. But then the smell filled my nose, overpowering the doctor's perfume, the disinfectant odor in the room; every other scent faded under the stench of blood.

And I puked.

Once my stomach had voided the small amount of liquid it held—I'd chugged bottled water on the drive over —I dry-heaved for a while.

With nose pinched and hand covering my mouth, I pointed at the blood without looking at it. "Hey, could you get rid of it? Please?" I swallowed, trying not to heave again.

I hadn't realized that during all of my heaving the big guy had left. But thankfully he returned now with a mop bucket that exuded a strong chemical odor and began mopping up the mess. He didn't look very happy about it.

"Why would you do that?" I asked the doctor with my hand still over my nose and mouth.

I swallowed and tried not to gag again. The odor was muted but it was still there. I leaned to my left, trying to see past Mr. Clean as he wielded the mop.

"The blood?" she asked. "It's part of the test."

I gave her an exasperated look. "You didn't get how squeamish I am when you drew my blood? You really needed to test that?"

Although that wasn't entirely true. Usually it was my own blood that made me cringe. And, weirdly, I *knew* that blood hadn't been mine. I didn't linger on *how* exactly I knew that.

She looked as annoyed with me as I felt, and she practically snapped, "Vampires aren't afraid of blood."

I considered whether I'd heard her correctly, decided I hadn't, and then decided I had. And that was it. I doubled over, and I laughed till I cried.

I laughed so hard that my side started to cramp up—and I kept laughing.

Several minutes later, my hand firmly clutching my aching side, I looked up to find Dr. Dobrescu standing alone near the door. Again, the big guy had managed to leave without me noticing—and this time with a huge yellow janitor's bucket on wheels. He was a sneaky one.

"You're a vampire." She said as if by making the statement sound factual, it was somehow less ridiculous.

"No. I'm not. You're certifiable."

She clutched that darn clipboard close to her body, like a shield. Against me. The vampire. "You are."

"I'm not. And I'm not going to play that game. Vampires aren't real. And clearly you're not a real doctor. Did you even go to medical school?"

Dr. Dobrescu named a prestigious medical school on the West Coast.

"Oh." I looked around the very normal office, with its normal exam table and normal posters. There were even those little canisters with cotton balls in them. "Well, maybe you're a doctor, but that doesn't mean you're not crazy."

She sighed. "How did you lose twenty-five pounds in a handful of days?"

"Starvation and a crazy-fast metabolism." Obviously. Never mind that the same question had been burbling around in my head since I woke from my comatose state.

She raised her eyebrows.

"What? That could happen." That so could *not* happen. "When's Mr. Clean coming back? Because I will not go quietly if you try to commit me. Or—" I made a stabbing motion. "You know, stake me."

Dr. Dobrescu's eyes grew large in her face. I thought I'd finally managed to shock her. Because me being a vampire hadn't done it. A vampire. Come on.

"Anton has determined that you're not currently a safety risk."

"*I'm* not a safety risk? What about you? With your blood vials and your weird bedside manner, not to mention your delusions."

Dr. Dobrescu stepped further into the room, gave me a speculative look, then came to some conclusion—because her attitude changed. She looked less businesslike. A little droopy, even. She sat down on the little rolling chair that all exam rooms seem to come equipped with and rolled closer to the table.

She assumed a solemn expression. "I am very sorry to have to tell you this, but you're no longer human. A virus has invaded your body, resulting in certain...changes."

Virus—that was a word I could grab hold of. Chew on a little. A scary word—but not a crazy one. The rest... My brain did a little la-la-la to the rest of what she was saying. "So what's the prognosis?"

I skipped over the fact that I was asking for medical information from a woman who had clearly lost her marbles.

"Unknown. The disease will most likely progress quite rapidly, but the end result is...uncertain. It's my under-standing that vampires require blood to complete the trans-formation."

"I'm sorry, did you say transformation?" I narrowed my eyes. "And what do you mean 'uncertain'?" I looked around the room. I was in a doctor's office and a doctor was telling me I might croak from a disease that didn't exist. Couldn't exist. Because when a doctor says the prognosis is uncertain —that has to include the big "D." Dead. Then I remem-bered: crazy lady talking. I swallowed a groan. Transforma-tion meant transformation into an undead vampire. "Are we talking about me ceasing to breathe, turning into a bat, and being afraid of garlic and crosses?"

Now she was looking at me like *I* was the crazy one.

I gritted my teeth and tried again. "When you say trans-formation, do you mean I will join the ranks of the undead?"

Good grief. If ever there was a phrase I never would have thought would pass my lips, that one scored in the top ten.

"Possibly. But there's also the very real possibility of regular dead. Not undead dead, just dead dead." Then she winced. "Your life in any form might end."

"Because I'm not into sucking blood? You have got to be kidding me. And, by the way, I feel fine. So how can you know what exactly this virus is doing to me?"

Mumbo jumbo doctor stuff followed, but the best I could understand, my body was supposedly going through some sort of transformation—the improved appearance of my skin, as well as other as yet undiscovered "perks"—and that this transformation was supposed to be fueled in part by the consumption of large quantities of blood.

"Hold on. I'm not"—my gag reflex kicked in, and I swallowed—"drinking blood. That is beyond disgusting."

"That's just it—if you can't consume blood, you'll starve. I suspect that had something to do with your rapid weight loss."

"Can't you just inject me? Give me a transfusion?"

"I don't think so. Humans can't digest blood, and vamps have to digest it to obtain—whatever they need from it. I'm a human doctor, and not an expert on vampirism. I'm only aware of the condition because of an incident with a client a few weeks ago. Anton was assigned to handle the resulting situation." Dr. Dobrescu crossed her arms.

And for only the second time since I'd stepped into the office, I noticed her. Not her lab coat or clipboard, but her. Fair-skinned with dark hair and light eyes. She didn't *look* like a crazy person.

"So, I'll suck it up and drink some blood." I choked back the hysterical giggle on the tip of my tongue. Who knew I'd get all punny when confronted with my own mortality?

"I don't think it's going to be that simple, but I hope it is. I hope I'm wrong. Again, I'm no expert—I only know what I've been told recently—and how to test for the virus."

"And who to contact if there's a safety risk." That phrase had an ominous ring to it. Then it hit me that I was inches from being designated one. "What would Anton have done if I had been a safety risk?"

The doc looked uncomfortable. Great—that couldn't be good.

"Well, is there at least a how-to manual? Do I get a

mentor? A consultant? Anything?" I scrubbed my face with both hands, then peeked between them to look at the doctor. Her green eyes looked kindly back. "I've drunk the Kool-Aid."

She reached into her lab coat pocket and pulled out a business card. "Anton is a member of the Society. They're your best resource for information on the virus and what to expect. Until I have more time...I just don't know very much. And since I'm not one of you, the Society isn't making what information they have available to me." Once I'd taken the card, she tilted her head. "Ah, he did say if you feel a murderous rage coming on, call the number on the back."

I accepted the card. "A murderous rage?"

Looking down, I found that she'd handed me a thick cream card, reminiscent of the old-style calling cards. It read simply: Anton. And underneath was a local number. I flipped it over to find a hastily scrawled number following the letters ER. Emergency room? Emergency? Ernest Riddle? Elijah Rockford? Some other random guy's name with the initials ER?

With a sinking feeling, I realized I'd bought in completely. The freakish smell of the blood, my reaction to it, my bizarre symptoms...it all meant something. And I *was* different. On some fundamental level, I had changed. Like a knot inside me had loosened.

"They don't expect me to last past a few days, do they?" I asked.

"I honestly don't know."

But I did. Because if this was all real, if I really was on the cusp of vampirism, then I had to be a huge security risk. I could blab to anyone. Or could I? Because who would believe me? I scrubbed my face again.

"Any last words of advice, doc?"

"Since it seems you can hold down water, that's a good place to start. And I guess experiment with what you can tolerate." She rolled her chair away and stood up. "And call the number. I truly hope they can help you."

As we walked down the hall together, she stopped suddenly. "I can't believe that I almost forgot. Your condition has to be kept secret. There are consequences for sharing the information broadly. Or with your family. Or your friends. It's best to just keep it to yourself."

"Yep—I figured that."

Dr. Dobrescu was about to walk me out the door of her clinic without taking any payment—or answering the tens of questions I suddenly realized I hadn't asked. The most pressing one popped out as we approached the exit. "How did I catch this virus?"

She raised her eyebrows, surprised by the question. "You were bitten."

Dr. Dobrescu pushed me out the door then shut it firmly, me on one side and her on the other.

5

MOTHER KNOWS (ME) BEST

The clouds gathered and the sky darkened. Like my mood. As I reached my car, the first fat drops were falling. The droplets beaded up nicely on my freshly waxed car.

I really didn't like that car.

The low-slung seat had always been difficult to get into, and, if anything, I was more agile now, but it annoyed me. Might be time to get a different car.

I drove home thinking about the doctor's visit. Why hadn't Anton given me the news if he was a part of the Society and the expert about vampires? Was he a vampire? Was the Society going to be the new "in" crowd? Another place I'd never fit in? And did I really care if I was just going to keel over in a matter of days?

"Nuts." I smacked my hand against the steering wheel. That was why Anton hadn't gone to any trouble with me. Because my sad, little broken self wasn't worth the effort to save. "Why not let the little weirdo who can't drink blood croak? If she happens to survive on her own, we'll have a chat with her. The nasty, slimy little toad."

A chill creeped across my skin. What if I told someone? What if I leaked the big secret and someone actually believed me? I'd bet dollars to dimes Anton would show up and do something *then*.

If my alternating peevishness and terror were any indication, I'd fully embraced this alternate reality—this really crummy alternate reality in which it was very possible that I didn't live much longer.

I really didn't get how I was supposed to be so horribly ill. I felt fine. Thirsty—but otherwise great. I glanced around the car—but I'd wiped out my bottled water stash already.

I was pretty wrapped up in my personal drama—dying was not an everyday occurrence for me—and I was *really* thirsty, so it was no shock that I missed a turn on my way home. The clinic was in south Austin, and I was a downtown girl. I didn't know the area at all, and my GPS had decided it needed to fritz as I was cruising through the unexplored wilds of south Austin.

I ended up meandering through a small neighborhood as my GPS flashed "rerouted" and provided no alternate route.

"Well look at you, you little darling." I pulled my snazzy red sports car to the curb and pulled out my phone. In the drive was some kind of Jeep—rugged and fun—with a for sale sign in the window. I dialed the number.

And twenty minutes later, I was the new owner of a Jeep Grand Cherokee. I hadn't known what a Cherokee was until today, but heck—if I only had a few days to live, I might as well drive a car I liked. I called the Audi dealer and made arrangements to have my other car picked up at the house of Mr. Saldana, the nice gentleman who sold me the car. An exceptionally nice man—and trusting; he took a personal check.

Mr. Saldana, or Michael, as he insisted I call him, spent a few minutes reviewing the basic features of the car and I was off in my nifty little boxy almost-truck. It was perfect.

My GPS finally cooperated, and I resumed the trek home. Not five minutes into the drive, my phone rang. I checked it, hoping and worrying it might be work. Maybe they had an unsolvable problem and needed me.

But no. It was my mother.

"Hi, Mother."

"Darling, how are you?" But in her typical style, she didn't wait for an answer. "I've called to ask you to accompany me to a luncheon. Since your father's death—" She paused for dramatic effect. It certainly wasn't grief. The man had died five years previous as they were in the midst of a nasty divorce. "Well, you know how much I dislike attending these functions on my own."

"Does Francesca have other plans?" My mother's go-to tennis and bridge buddy, Francesca enjoyed the outings, which was why Mom usually asked her first. I was her last-ditch choice.

"Dear, Francesca and I aren't spending as much time together these days." Mom sniffed. "She's dating a *very* young man. I do not approve."

"Hm. Mother, can I call you back when I get home? I just picked up a new car and I should probably be paying closer attention."

"Oh, but your lease on the Audi isn't up yet, is it? Did you have an accident? Are you all right? Why didn't you call?" This time she did wait for a response after her barrage of questions. Because as annoying as my mother could be, the woman did love me.

"I'm fine." No need to expound upon the vampire thing. If I was dying, I wasn't spending my last few days in a mental institution. Or being hunted down by Mr. Clean. A tiny spark of an idea was forming in my head as to how I might spend those days. "The Audi doesn't suit me any longer. I bought a Jeep. A preowned Jeep."

And I waited for it.

Silence followed.

I could practically feel the shock. The surprise. I bit my lip to keep from giggling.

"But it's been used. By someone else."

"That is what preowned means, Mother." I watched the dust motes dance in the sunlight. "I'm sure the previous owner thoroughly cleaned it before they put it up for sale."

Best not to mention the minor hail damage or the colorful Kinky Friedman bumper sticker.

"Are you sure you're all right? You don't sound like yourself. And it's just so hard to imagine you in a...a *used* car."

"I'm good. I feel lighter. Like I've shed a burden." And I didn't mean that twenty-five pounds. "I'm freer."

"Honey, you're not high, are you? I know there's a lot pressure at work and lots of the kids do it—"

"Mother, stop. I'm thirty-nine. I'm not influenced by what the *kids* are doing."

"You know what I mean—so you're not taking drugs?"

Mom sounded so concerned that I almost offered to go to that luncheon with her—but then I realized I couldn't see her. We'd had lunch just a few weeks ago. She'd never believe how much weight I'd lost. Fake tanner would be an easy enough explanation for my newly even skin. Mom had recommended it often enough—but there was no easy fix for my weight loss. "No, definitely not taking drugs."

"Oh, I know—it's a man, isn't it? You've finally met someone!"

"No. Have to run. New car, driving..." No need for her to

know I was in light traffic and having no difficulties with the new dashboard controls. "Bye now."

"All right. Let's talk soon, though." Mom sounded a little forlorn, but she did finally hang up.

The rest of my drive home was uneventful, except for three rather startling realizations that occurred almost one after the other.

I was moving to the 'burbs. The little detour I'd taken through the south Austin neighborhood where I'd found my new car had appealed even more than my new ride. I'd worked hard my whole life, didn't spend extravagantly, had saved—and my home didn't feel like much of a home. I wasn't really excited about moving, but living somewhere like the tiny neighborhood where I'd found my new car— that appealed.

Which led to my next realization. I used to love my apartment. The sparseness of it let me keep a clear head. I'd been able to breathe in that apartment. But now it felt bare —barren, even.

I used to love my Audi, but clearly that ship had sailed. And my clothes. I was wearing a T-shirt I usually slept in. And that conversation with my mother.

I was the same person as I'd been a week ago—but somehow different. It was like a whole heap of insecurities and fears had fled. I wasn't worried about going broke—I could spend a little money. Granted, retirement seemed a little pointless with a death sentence hanging over my head. And the untidiness of a house in the suburbs seemed appealing—because I'd have my own tiny patch of grassy yard. And maybe roses. I'd like some roses. The idea of dirt and bugs didn't make my scalp crawl—so yeah, roses would be great.

But the last realization was the most important. I was

hunting down the rat who'd bitten me and screwed with my life. Or, rather, the vampire. Whatever he was, I was hunting him down.

6

RATS VS. THE FLU

I was gonna hunt down the vile vampire rat who'd bitten me...just as soon as I could get out of bed. I'd made it home in my spiffy new car—and then my energy level had crashed. Maybe I should have tried to eat? Or maybe I should have drunk another gallon of water? Or even orange juice? And I didn't sleep-drink this time, because I forgot to fill the pitcher next to my bed before collapsing.

When I woke, the sun was up—so I'd slept at least twelve hours. Given my past experiences, it was likely longer. And as I lay there, my regrets were piling up. I felt horrendous, and getting out of bed seemed impossible. The achiness was back. The coma-like sleep, back. The raging thirst, back. I had graduated from the crusty goo that had accumulated in my eyes before—so a bonus there. That was my last thought before I drifted off a second time, too weak to make a bathroom or kitchen run for emergency hydration.

My stomach felt empty, but I rolled over and slept. It nagged, made my sleep restless. It hurt, made me toss and turn. It burned. Angry. Demanding.

I woke to piercing, gut-churning pain.

My lips cracked when I opened my mouth to moan. Curled in on myself and clutching my stomach, I couldn't see how this could get worse.

No one was coming to check on me. My phone wasn't near. And I hurt like crazy. Maybe this was it. Maybe a day was all I'd had. Nuts. I should be terrified, but I just felt pathetic. I was that alone, that isolated. No one would miss me.

I concentrated on breathing. Even, slow breaths. It worked for a few seconds, then a wave of hungry pain washed through me.

A few breaths, and I rolled to the edge of the bed.

A few more breaths, and I rolled off the bed.

The jarring pain as I hit the floor was nothing compared to the spasms in my gut. The sting cleared my head, and I began to crawl—foot by foot—to the bathroom.

Water. Maybe it would help. Or maybe this was it, and nothing I did could help me. I waited for the crushing weight of despair...but I was just too tired to feel that much.

After a few minutes of waiting, I realized that I wasn't *that* tired. Dying was bad. Super bad. Dead-not-waking-up bad. I couldn't just curl up and let it happen. I had to try. So I crawled, inch by inch, to the bathroom.

The tile felt cold under my thigh, my hip, my cheek. I didn't feel hot—but the floor was icy.

I couldn't stand. The tub faucet was so close—I pulled at the knob and water splashed...too far to drink.

WHEN I WOKE, I was hungry. Pit-of-my-stomach-gnawing hunger. But I didn't hurt. Even the flu-like ache was gone. I cracked my eyes open but quickly clenched them tightly shut again when the light stung them. I lifted my hand reflexively, but when it touched my face, it was wet.

Cautiously this time, I opened my eyes again. I was in my bathtub. The tub was almost full. So full, I couldn't believe I hadn't drowned.

I remembered turning the water on...but that was it. Getting in the tub, turning the water off—that was all a blank.

I hadn't stripped, since I still wore the tennis skirt and T-shirt I'd put on—how many days ago? Good lord. There was no way I still had a job.

Standing was difficult, but I managed to prop myself against the wall. As I stood, water sloshed over the edge of the tub. I truly didn't know how I'd gotten into the tub given the state I was in, or how I'd avoided drowning myself in the full tub while comatose.

I stepped out and stripped. I was still pretty drained, and wearing a bunch of wet clothes wasn't helping. As I turned to leave the bathroom, I caught my profile in the mirror. "Ack!"

Frozen in front of the mirror, an emaciated version of my former self stared back. Where I'd thought my face gaunt before, it was clear it had merely been sharply defined. *This* was gaunt. The hollows under my cheeks had deepened. My face was all eyes, cheekbones, nose, and chin, with no flesh to round it out. It was grotesque. *I* was grotesque.

Because the sight had startled me, it took a moment for me to see that my lips were not just chapped and cracked. I had two very distinct cuts on my bottom lip, both equal distances from the corner of my mouth. My breath quickened and I stepped closer to the mirror—to the stranger in the mirror.

I opened my mouth...

Relief welled up inside me and escaped as a single, choked laugh. No fangs. No oddly sharp teeth. Just my teeth. That, at least, hadn't changed.

I turned away from the image in the mirror and marched to the kitchen. Time to do a little digging and some eating. Because I could hardly deny that starvation was just around the corner. That—and I was hungry enough to eat cardboard.

I grabbed my laptop on the way. Online research was definitely my next step.

Laptop open on the kitchen table, I reached for my first experiment. Orange juice. I'd tried it and puked it before—but had it been the orange juice or the peanut butter or the bread that had triggered my puking fit? That was the question.

I gulped down some OJ, then belatedly realized I should have measured it. Measuring cup in hand, it occurred to me that I should also be timing this little gastro-experiment. I set the timer to fifteen minutes, because I was pretty sure my adverse reaction had asserted itself within that time frame. Which sparked my next brilliant idea: a handy metal bowl. Portable and dishwasher safe—the perfect repository should one of my experiments fail.

While I waited for the contents to settle—or not—I pulled up what I could find on the constituent components of human blood. And what supported good blood health.

And my stomach kept reminding me—*I'm hungry, wench. Feed me.*

So I didn't quite make it to fifteen minutes. At five, I decided OJ by itself had qualified as a winner, and I finished

off the carton. I set the timer for another five minutes—
because that was apparently my max tolerance for intense
hunger while standing in a kitchen not quite devoid of food.

I dug around in the fridge and found squat, so I shifted
my attention to the cupboard. Dried apricots, maybe.
Almonds sounded delish. Coffee beans. Yum. I started a
kettle of boiling water.

The timer dinged my five-minute reprieve, and I stuffed
an apricot in my mouth. Now was as good a time as any for
the odd bits in my fridge to go, so I pulled out the squishy
tomato and chucked it in the bin. Immediately thereafter,
with an accuracy I wish I could claim as intentional, I threw
up in that same bin.

I suspected the apricot—but I couldn't be sure. That was
when I discovered the flaw in my less-than-well-prepared
plan. Was it the OJ and a delayed reaction? Or the apricot
and an immediate one? Was it a combination of both?

The singing of my kettle interrupted my self-flagellation.
I dithered for a spare minute—then decided that I might as
well give coffee a whirl.

Thirty minutes later, I hugged the bag of coffee beans
close to my chest and danced a little jig. Then I might
possibly have run a few laps in my small apartment, yelled,
"Hallelujah," and then ordered fifty pounds of coffee online.
Possibly. To be delivered immediately. I might have
done that.

7

GETTING A LIFE

Step one in moving my life forward required me to have a life. The kind where my heart continued to beat and my lungs filled with air. I didn't really believe I was going to die. First, I didn't feel *that* bad. And second, death was big. Huge. And I was thirty-nine. I wasn't ready to die, so I couldn't be dying. Denial? Definitely. But if it got me out of bed, I'd take it.

And now that I was not only out of bed, but had also discovered my vampiric drug of choice (coffee), and had found a few tidbits that I could eat...or drink, I was ready to find my life, wherever it might lurk.

I flipped the plain cream-colored card over. To call Anton, the sneaky rat who couldn't be bothered to explain what I was, how I was supposed to live, and why this had happened to me. Hm. Or to call the mysterious ER.

The obnoxious and heartless unknown or the mysterious and even more unknown.

I considered for about a tenth of a second and dialed the number for ER. Anton could stick it.

After two rings, a man answered. "Where are you?"

His abruptness caught me off guard, and I said, "At home. Where are you?"

I held the phone away from my face, winced over my idiocy, then put the phone back next to my ear.

I'd clearly missed something, because there was silence. "Hello? Sorry—I missed that?"

"What is your emergency?" The guy sounded more than a little put out.

"Are you kidding me? I'm a...a...you know, with the blood and the bats and the crosses."

"I'm tracing this call. We have a zero-tolerance policy for crank callers."

Good grief. Maybe Anton would have been better. "I'm not a crank caller. I'm a..."

A sigh came across the line. "A vampire?"

"Yes!" I hadn't realized how hard it would be to say that out loud. Especially over the phone, to someone who would likely think I was a crazy lady.

"What is the nature of your emergency?"

He was clearly losing his patience, but he wasn't the only one.

"I just told you. I'm a vampire. That is the nature of my emergency."

"Are you experiencing an uncontrolled bloodlust?"

I threw up a little in my mouth. "No, definitely not."

"Are you experiencing the onset of a murderous rage?"

I stopped and considered that one. I hadn't been. I might be now. "No, although you might push me over the edge."

"Look, lady. I'm on a date—with a very hot woman I've been trying to get to go out with me for a long time. You've interrupted my extremely hot date with your emergency call. If you can't tell me what the nature of your emergency is, I'm hanging up."

"I'm a recently turned vampire who can't eat blood, is about two steps away from starving, and no one gives a rat's rear about it. On top of that, some vile fanged guy bit and infected me, and I'm not supposed to call the cops because it's all hush-hush with the paranormal freaky stuff. But even if I wanted to call the po-po, no luck there, because I haven't a clue who stuck their tiny, cowardly, inadequate fangs in me. But wait—when I finally call someone I think might be able to help me, a horny teenager who can't be bothered to give me the time of day answers." I took a giant breath. "My *life* is an emergency."

Silence.

"Hellooo?"

"Give the horny teenager a break. That was a mouthful to digest." He sounded slightly less annoyed with me. "Where did you get this number?"

I growled. "Mr. Clean passed the card to my doctor, who then passed it to me."

The horny teen responded with a deep chuckle. Maybe not a teenager after all. "That sounds like Anton. We must have been short-handed, or you have some terrible luck, lady. What's your name?"

Finally—a reasonable question. "Mallory. And I am sorry to interrupt your date."

"Yeah, well, you and me both—but I'm on call, so it's not completely unexpected. Are you in any immediate danger?"

"About that—every time I fall asleep, I wake up significantly diminished. In size. As in, I'm losing weight really fast."

"Yeah. If you can't consume blood and you're going through the transformation... Ah, you said you went to the doctor and that's where you met Anton?"

"Right. But my doctor was clueless. Other than telling

me to try drinking lots of water and wishing me luck, she couldn't get me gone fast enough. Oh, and telling me I'm probably toast. Sorry—not long for this earth. Not in so many words, but basically. Although other than being really hungry—no bloodlust, just really hungry—I feel fine. And the coffee has really helped."

A choking noise sounded on the line. "Don't drink coffee."

"What? It makes me feel great. And it's one of the few things I can get down."

"Yeah, well, coffee makes most vamps a little nutty, so be cautious." Some background noise cut through, then I heard muffled voices—probably speaking to his smoking date. "If you think you can hang on till morning, I can swing by, pick you up, and take you in to see one of the Society vamps. If it helps, most vampires seem to drink whatever they want, but I've not seen one consume solids. So maybe give some other liquids besides coffee a try."

"Sure thing. Thank you. Oh, and good luck on your date."

"Cheers."

"Oh, wait a second. Hello?"

"Still here."

"Don't you need my address?"

"No joke about the crank-calling policy. I've got your address."

"Right. Got it." Because that wasn't creepy at all. "Thanks again!"

But he'd already hung up.

Now, to get through the night. No problem. Coffee didn't seem to make *me* nutty, so I'd just drink coffee all night. That way, I wouldn't fall asleep, and all the creepy transformation stuff that happened in my sleep couldn't happen.

🦇

Five hours later I was seeing music, hearing colors, and talking to my dead Great-Auntie Lula.

Can't drive. Can't call my mother. Noooooo. Definitely can't call Mother. Looking like a skeleton, talking like a crazy lady, I'd end up in an institution for sure.

I paced. Chugged some water. Paced.

Maybe some more coffee would be good. Noooo! No. More. Coffee. Bad me. Bad.

I paced some more. And then brilliance struck. "Shakes!" I looked at the fading figure of Great-Auntie Lula and waved as she faded away. "Thank you!"

Because Great-Auntie Lula had practically lived on this one particular brand of vegan nutrition supplement shakes the last few years of her life. I'd even tried them, and they weren't half bad.

"Now, where does an emaciated vamp strung out on caffeine go to get her vegan shake fix? Ha!" I knew right away. There was only one place where I wouldn't stick out like a sore thumb. One place that welcomed all comers at all hours.

I called a cab. I was going to Walmart.

8

NOT A PIMPLE IN SIGHT

Contrary to all my efforts, I did eventually fall asleep. I passed out on my sofa sometime around three or four in the morning in the midst of sorting donation-worthy clothes. Moving was the perfect opportunity to dump unneeded stuff, and my much, much too large clothing counted as unneeded.

I still wasn't sure what vampirism was: part science, part magic? In any event, it was one hundred percent weird. Because I consumed a greater quantity of supplement shakes, well into the wee hours of the night, than a human body could possibly handle.

I'd been hungry, and the shakes had "stuck," with the odd exception of chocolate. Chocolate was not a vamp's friend. Or at least not this vamp's.

I'd drunk so much I'd managed to fill out my cheeks a little. I'd even accomplished the herculean task of taking the edge off that nasty, aching hunger that seemed to have taken up residence in my gut.

And then I'd slept like the dead. An unfortunate turn of phrase, perhaps, but the one that came to mind at eight thirty when I was awoken by a pounding on my apartment door.

I blinked blearily and couldn't even stir up an ounce of shame over the strewn glasses, bags of donation clothing, and oddly placed boxes throughout the room. If you knocked on my door without warning, you deserved an eyeful of chaos.

I rolled out of bed surprisingly limber and completely ache-free. The day was looking up. I glanced down at my nightwear. The kids' T-shirt I'd picked up the night before had seemed appropriate at the time—and it had fit. In the light of the day, the giant mouse hugged my barely A-cup breasts in a somewhat salacious and completely inappropriate way. But it still made me want to do a little dance. I didn't have any boobs at all yesterday.

Maybe I wouldn't waste away into nothingness after all.

I glanced to make sure I had bottoms on—check—and opened the front door.

A tall guy with a little bit of dark scruff stood in the doorway. He had broad shoulders, but just normal-guy broad, not the variety that required hours and hours of dedicated gym time.

"Guy with the hot date. Nuts." The words tumbled out.

"Yeah, that didn't go to plan." He eyed my clothes. "You didn't answer when I called, so I came on up."

The security in the building was *supposed* to be really good. Then again—I was moving, so not quite so troubling. I'd have to mention the issue to Mrs. A, though.

"What was your name? I don't think I got it last night." I opened the door wide, inviting him inside.

He took a look around and then walked in. "Is this your usual look?"

"I'm moving. And might have had a little too much caffeine last night."

He grinned. "I told you about that. Any hallucinations?"

I gave him a squinty-eyed look. "You could have said. But yes. Unless ghosts are a thing, I was hallucinating left and right."

He tipped his head, neither affirming nor denying the existence of ghosts.

"Nooo." I crossed my arms. "Spill. Because if Great-Auntie Lula is planning to hang around a lot, I'd prefer to be prepared."

He examined the room, then said, "No spirits, and I don't think any ghosts have been in here lately either. I'm Alex." He extended his hand.

"No ghosts, huh?" I stuck my hand out.

When he shook my hand, I'd swear he flinched. But sometimes when you think the lights are flickering, you just blinked. This was probably the same.

"Who do you work for?" I asked.

"Myself. Do you mind if we chat while you get dressed? Or in the car?" He put his hands in his pockets. "I have some work to do later this afternoon."

"Ah." I glanced down at my clothes. Not exactly suitable for an outing. But as luck would have it, in my semi-deranged state the night previous, I'd had the foresight to pick up a few things that fit better than basically every other item of clothing I owned. "What's the dress for this place?"

Alex had on jeans and a plain, fitted T-shirt, but who knew if that was indicative of appropriate attire. Then again, I didn't have many options. A wraparound dress or jeans and a T-shirt.

He shrugged. "Whatever you like."

I went in the bathroom, washed my face, brushed my

57

teeth, and generally cleaned myself up. Although it was becoming increasingly clear that vamps didn't share the same hygiene requirements as humans. I didn't seem to actually sweat. Bizarre.

Another bizarre fact, intermittent starvation notwithstanding: I still had long, wavy, healthy hair. My skin had changed, but my hair was basically the same. I threw it up in a ponytail, and then dressed in the jeans and T-shirt. A little lipstick, my handy All Stars, and I was ready to go. At least my shoes still fit.

I was energized—but who knew how long that would last.

"Ready," I said as I popped out of my bedroom.

Alex was speaking quietly on his phone, but hung up as soon as he saw me. Not suspicious at all. "All right. The Society—that's the Society for the Study of Occult and Paranormal Phenomena—is located in southeast Austin. They have a warehouse space with a small retail front."

"I'm sorry—the Society...?"

"The Society for the Study of Occult and Paranormal Phenomena. Superficially, it's a club for hobbyists—but it's actually the front for an organization that governs the local community." He held up his keys.

"Sure." I grabbed my purse and keys. "Oh, I can drive. I have a new car." I couldn't help but feel a little chipper about the prospect of sharing my new ride. It gave me a case of the happies to even think about driving it. No idea why—but it did. "Oh, nuts. I need to call the dealership about my other car. I keep falling asleep, and time just gets away from me."

"I think that's temporary." Alex opened the door, not so subtly urging me to hurry.

I was in the hallway, not far from Mrs. A's door, when I

realized I didn't know what Alex was. I hurried past and then stopped once I'd escaped her peephole view. "If you're not one of me—what are you?"

"Thief, assassin, wizard—different people have different names for us." He kept walking.

"But what do you call yourself?"

He raised his eyebrows. "Alex."

"You had detention a lot as a kid, didn't you?"

"Basically." He pushed the elevator button, glanced at her keys, and said, "I'll drive."

"Fine, but you're putting a dent in my happy. I just got a new car."

He grinned. "A dent in your happy, huh? How about a compromise? I drive, but we can take your new car."

That was actually pretty decent of him to try to accommodate me. And while the thought of some strange man driving my car would have given me fits not long ago, in the moment, it seemed reasonable enough. I handed him my keys with a smile. "Thank you."

As we rode the elevator down in that awkward silence that only elevators seemed to promote, my mind started flipping through all of the odds and ends of my changing life. Find a lease management company for the apartment, find a new house, hire movers, change the title of my new car. My job—the thought buzzed through my brain, like a little, irritating mosquito. I should call them today.

I spoke into the abyss of silence. "I think I'm going to quit my job."

He must have been lost in his own thoughts, because it took him a second to focus on me. "Okay. Any particular reason?"

"Everyone there hates me. And I won't starve." I flashed him an insanely bright smile. Because when I said the words, I knew in my bones they were true. I wouldn't starve. I wouldn't be without a place to live. I wouldn't be broke in my old age—if I had one. But most important was the revelation that I didn't need that job to make my world go 'round. Hallelujah. "Yep. I'll call today."

He shifted. "Email."

"Sorry?"

"You should email. If you've been out for a while and don't have close ties—email is easier."

"Right. Email it is."

I saved my questions for the car ride, because the parking lot level teemed with shoppers and other foot traffic. The bottom level of the building was retail—another thing I wouldn't miss. The suburbs seemed so quiet. So peaceful.

Once we were underway, I asked, "What's the deal with Anton? He didn't say two words to me. He could have at least slipped me the secret handshake, hooked me up with a vamp mentor, something."

"Just to be clear, the vamp you're meeting today has agreed to speak with you, but I wouldn't consider him mentor material."

"That's okay—I'm just glad for some information. I'm like the little beggar waiting for scraps. This Society isn't very organized, is it? I mean, I'm running around town with no clue, for all anyone knows ready to blow the lid off vampirism in Austin, and they're sitting back watching it all happen. Not cool." I snapped my fingers. "I'd forgotten about the murderous rage thing. Anton had no idea I wasn't going to bust out in a murderous rage. He gave me a number, just in case I thought I might. Who does that?"

"He did have some idea. He'd met you, hadn't he? Besides, what do you think he should have done? Detained you illegally? Killed you before you could harm someone because you *might*?"

"Obviously I don't think that." I glanced at him to see if I'd made him angry, but all of his focus was on not hitting pedestrians as he drove through the parking garage.

"That's how it used to be. It's better now."

"I believe you. But that Anton guy still stinks."

Alex's lips twitched. "Anton doesn't particularly like vampires."

"So he's definitely not a vampire. What is he, then?"

"Assassin."

"Wait—he's like you?"

"Sort of. A little bigger, a little buffer."

I laughed. "A lot. He really did look like Mr. Clean."

He played it off like it was nothing, but Mr. Thief-Assassin-Wizard really didn't like to talk about his particular paranormal or occult leanings—to borrow the Society's nomenclature.

An unpleasant thought occurred. "Do you like vampires?"

He did glance my way this time. "Not usually."

"Ugh. Does anyone like vampires?"

Now he was grinning. "Other vampires?"

I huffed out an annoyed breath. I was among the Hated, and this time it wasn't even my fault. "That nasty little twerp that bit me deserves to be..." I was at a loss. What happened to people in this community who broke the rules?

"That is a death sentence."

"What—biting me?"

"Oh, no. Vamps need blood to survive. That's the traditional wisdom. Drinking deep isn't allowed without the Society's permission and participation. To screen potential converts and to prepare them." He merged on the highway.

"You are most definitely an accident, and, if caught, your progenitor will be hanged."

"Progenitor—that's what the contagious neck-raper who infected me is called?"

Alex cleared his throat. "Neck-raper? You might keep that one to yourself."

"Progenitor sounds like something from a science experiment. Not something furtive and dirty."

"Creating a new vamp usually isn't furtive and dirty—not anymore." He exited the freeway only a few miles south of downtown. "We're about seven minutes out."

"This place isn't that far from downtown." I'd been living in the downtown bubble for too long. Austin was broader than the few square miles of governmental buildings, live music venues, and high-rise townhouses that comprised downtown. Turning back to Alex, I couldn't help notice he was a very nice-looking man. "So tell me about your date."

He glanced at me, then his eyes turned back to the road. "No."

"Come on. You said she was hot. Where did you meet her?"

He ignored the question.

"Okay. What about your job—you said you work for yourself."

Silence.

"I'm going to think your racism is affecting your social skills."

"Racism?" He'd pulled into an area full of warehouses. "You're a vamp. That doesn't change your race."

Maybe a direct question... "What exactly do you do, working for yourself?"

"When I offered to introduce you, I don't remember agreeing to a personal interview."

"Not racist...maybe a misogynist?" I watched and waited for some response. An actual misogynist would probably be pissed.

He smiled. "Okay, if you say so."

This conversation was proving much less illuminating than I'd hoped.

"And it's not an interview; it's called small talk. People do it every day. You should practice a little. A little small talk might get you further on your next hot date."

His lips twitched up into a cocky smile. "I said the date didn't go to plan—not that it didn't go far."

"Ick. Did you just tell me you got laid? TMI."

He laughed. "You wanted small talk." The Jeep came to a halt. "We're here."

And indeed we were. The Society for the Study of Occult and Paranormal Phenomena had a huge sign. I blinked and looked again. Not just a sign, but window displays. "Is that fake blood? Please say yes." I could feel my face squishing up.

"Relax. Completely fake. The real stuff's in the back."

"Oh, no. That is so gross. Don't tell me you have fridges filled with the stuff back there?"

"Okay, I won't tell you that. Come on—Wembley's van is here. No telling how long he's been waiting."

I hesitated with one foot out of the car. "Didn't you tell me that no one likes vampires? Should I be worried about meeting this guy?"

"No, not at all. Wembley's cool." When I gave him a suspicious look, he shrugged. "He's the exception. A while ago, his life took a sharp left turn, and he's been pretty agreeable since then. He's kind of an odd guy."

The implication being that I would get along fabulously with him, since I also was a weirdo. Gee whiz—thanks.

9

MY FIRST REAL VAMPIRE EVER

Alex escorted me through a retail area filled with capes, fake fangs, tarot cards, religious votive candles, gemstones, witch hats, green and black hair dye, a display case with crucifixes, and yes—fake blood. He nodded at the cute teenage girl who was manning the register, and she waved back with a besotted smile.

I wasn't the only one to find something enticing about Alex. Maybe it was his accountant turned bad boy looks. Hm. I wouldn't have thought he would have such broad appeal.

I leaned down to get a better look at the shrunken head on one of the shelves. "This place has a bizarre combo of merchandise. Spiritual mixed in with kitschy sprinkled with Halloween festive."

"And all in a store for a group that purports to 'study' paranormal and the occult. I know. Over time, the store has taken on a life of its own."

"Right..." I backed away from a display case of stakes, holy water, and dried garlic necklaces. They didn't *seem* dangerous—but what did I know about my new body?

Maybe I was deathly allergic to garlic. Although they wouldn't have something that was poisonous to vamps in a retail store fronting the Society. Would they?

I stepped on Alex's foot. "Oh, sorry."

Standing a hairsbreadth from my back, he grasped my upper arms and steadied me then stepped away. "That stuff can't hurt you. Well, don't fall on the stake, but otherwise you should be good."

I could feel myself blushing. Which was ridiculous. How was I supposed to know what was dangerous and what wasn't?

Alex was waiting patiently a few feet away next to a door marked "Employees Only." Just like any other retail store.

"Sorry." But I couldn't help frowning at him, and I wasn't sure why I was apologizing.

He didn't comment, just opened the door for me.

As I stepped closer, I saw a security pad above the door-knob. Not quite like most retail stores, then. Alex must have punched in the code when I wasn't looking. That was twice now that he'd been Mr. Stealthy where security systems were in question. I needed to quiz this Wembley guy about thief-assassin-wizards.

I took a breath and steeled myself for my first real-life vampire meeting. I had to stifle a giggle when I realized *I* was my first real-life vampire.

When I hesitated, Alex walked through the door, and I followed him into a dark hallway.

"The second door on the right. That leads to the lounge and the most likely place for Wembley to be waiting."

I hesitated. "We're not going to walk in on him partaking, are we?"

"In a bloody Mary, maybe." When I refused to move forward, even with his hand at my elbow urging me forward, he added, "No, Wembley will not be consuming blood in any form. I told him about your phobia."

"Not a phobia. A life choice."

"It's a life choice for you to avoid blood?" He walked to the door and opened it. "Come on. He won't bite."

"Ha-ha. So funny." But it was just a little. And it got my feet moving.

I walked through the door and into another decade. I stumbled, caught my balance, and then stood still, blinking.

Oranges, pinks, and purples competed for dominance. The walls were a deep, rich shade of purple. The sofa was orange, with pink accent pillows. Candles of pink, purple, and orange abounded—but there were also blues and greens. A bright pink lava lamp, an orange beanbag chair, and purple bong complemented the decor. In the corner, all variety of colored beads hung from the ceiling, creating a curtain across the entryway into a small kitchen nook.

"Too much? It was my turn to decorate, and I couldn't resist the urge to travel back in time." A middle-aged, slightly paunchy, grey-bearded guy with longish hair and rose-tinted glasses spread his hands wide. "Jefferson Wembley, at your service."

He didn't offer his hand, so I followed his lead.

"Mallory Andrews."

He indicated the sofa. "Have a seat. Can I get you a drink?" Before I could respond, Wembley turned to Alex. "Get lost, buddy. We're going to talk about the Man, and I know how you get."

Alex shook his head. "I need to do a little work, so you can catch me in my office when you're done."

After he left, I asked Wembley from the very deep seat of the sofa, "What exactly is it that he does?"

"He owns Bits, Baubles, and Toadstools." At my confused look, Wembley said, "The shop out front."

I rolled my eyes. Alex could have just said.

"He's also one of the Society's enforcers."

I was still shaking my head at Alex's annoyingly and unnecessarily secretive behavior when "enforcer" penetrated my brain. "I'm sorry—enforcer? I thought he was, like, the Society's equivalent of a paramedic."

Wembley's eyes widened. "Sure. If you believe the man." He dropped down onto the beanbag chair.

Wembley's reasoning defied logic.

"Wembley—is that right? Or do you prefer Jefferson?"

"No one's called me Jefferson since... I'm not actually sure that anyone has ever called me Jefferson. Wembley, please."

"Right. Wembley. If by the man, you mean the Society, you do realize you're chilling out in a lounge inside the Society's headquarters?"

His shaggy eyebrows waggled, and he shifted forward in the beanbag chair. "You think it's bugged?"

"No. I'm saying, for a guy who is against the man, you seem pretty comfortable in his lounge."

Wembley chuckled. "L-e-m-a-n-n. Sounds a lot like 'the man.' He's the CSO for the Society and who Alex reports to when he's wearing his emergency response hat."

"Emergency response? Oh..." I pulled Anton's card out of my purse. Handing it to Wembley, I asked, "ER means emergency response?"

Wembley glanced at the front, flipped it to the back, then returned it. "That's right. The number is answered by on-call staff. There are a handful of knights—enforcers—and the rest are administrative staff."

"So what do these emergency response people do?" I

didn't get nearly the weird creepy vibe from "emergency response" that I did from "enforcer."

"Ostensibly? They offer aid to the community when we can't call the police." Wembley squinted. "You do know we're all hush-hush underground, right?"

"Yep. I got that. What do you *think* the ER folks do?"

"Well, with seven knights answering calls, I think it's about cover-ups and cleanups—what else? Alex isn't so bad, but knights are a sketchy bunch. All about swords and violence, retribution and order. That kind of thing."

Something niggled in the back of my brain. "The hangings..."

"Hm. Yes. But you're talking about lawful execution. I'm talking about what happens to those outside the formal justice system. Before it ever gets to a fair trial. But I could be wrong—you're here, after all."

I tried for a poker face—but failed utterly. I could feel my eyes get wide. "Why would I not be here?"

"Oh, back in the old days, the Society would have disappeared you."

"But now they just ignore me and hope for the best? That hardly sounds like a good plan for the health of the community." Great—I was talking like Wembley. Like I even knew who made up "the community."

Wembley steepled his fingers together, a gesture at odds with his slumped posture in the beanbag chair. "I don't think you were expected to survive. You're an anomaly. If you don't mind me asking—how exactly are you feeding yourself? You have an aversion to blood, correct?"

Every time I thought about blood, I had a flashback to the doctor's office and that noxious smell.

"I've never been able to watch when my blood's been drawn, but I've never actually been phobic. Then the doctor shoved a tube of blood in my hand, and I freaked out and dropped it even though it wasn't mine and it was in a tube." A shiver crawled across my skin. "Pretty sure that was all about Anton confirming something was up with me."

He leaned forward. "Quite possibly."

I shrank back into the depths of the sofa. "Uh..." I pointed as discreetly as I could at his mouth, where a wicked set of fangs had appeared. "Your, uh, you know..."

Quick as a flash, the fangs disappeared. "Ah. I was fasting—good for the spleen and all that—when Alex contacted me about this meeting. I'm somewhat susceptible to the odd suggestion right now. You were saying about the blood?"

There was still a glint in his eye at the mention of blood —but no fangs.

"Well, the odor was terrible. Noxious. I can't describe it. I was too busy puking to take notes."

"The smell of blood made you vomit. Blood certainly shouldn't trigger an aversive reaction in a vampire. So fascinating." He eyed me like I was a tiny little lab rat.

"That's all you have to say? No explanations? Advice? Anything?"

Wembley smiled. "You're here, so you're obviously eating something. What's keeping you going?"

This was certainly turning out to be less informative than I'd hoped. Was it too much to ask that my own people know how to keep me alive? And maybe share that information with me?

I sighed. "Vegan nutrition supplement shakes, orange juice, tons of water, and some coffee. Though after about three large French-press pots, I got a little loopy." Looking around the room, I added, "It might be something you'd enjoy. I saw some weird stuff. But before that last pot—it was heavenly."

"Hm." Wembley gave me a curious look. "Not decaf?"

"You're kidding, right? Why bother?" I tried not to look at him like he was a crazy man—but decaffeinated coffee? Why not just pee in a cup and drink that? At least that wouldn't taste like some chemically manufactured cocktail.

"Well, most vamps would be trying to fly off the top of a very tall building by the second or third cup. Your reaction is odd, just so you know."

"Oh." I tried to remember what exactly I'd experienced. "My painting spoke to me, Great-Auntie Lula appeared—she was the key, because she used to drink Ensure shakes all day. Although Alex seemed pretty sure no real ghosts had been in my place. And there was the car alarm that smelled like burnt bacon, the neighbor's music that smelled like lilacs, and the freaky feeling of falling when I opened the bathroom door. Generally, very trippy."

"Interesting. Very, very interesting."

I raised my hands in the universal gesture that meant: tell me what you know, you secret-hoarding devil.

"Yes, well"—again with the steepling fingers—"every vamp has certain talents that develop during the transformation. Perhaps you have a touch of precognition. Less common than telepathy—which also is quite rare—but they're believed to be related gifts."

"Precognition, as in seeing the future? It didn't seem like that at all. Not like a vision or anything."

"It's typically very subtle. An unidentifiable preference for a specific seat in a restaurant that results in a glass of wine not spilling on you—that type of thing. It can be exciting stuff, even if it isn't always useful." Wembley waggled his bushy eyebrows again. "And in your case, you might get some decent mileage out of it if you're getting those kinds of tips. Telepathy is a bit more straightforward, but again, usually only the lowest levels of talent occur—like getting a strong feeling that someone is angry or sad. You're not getting any of that, though, are you? Just the precog, right?"

"Definitely no hints as to what people are thinking." My experience with the Jeep came to mind. "I did have this bizarre urge to buy a new car. It makes me ridiculously happy to drive it. Not a clue why. Maybe the precognition you're talking about?"

"That's what I mean. You'll just have to see if it develops into a more usable talent. Are there any other peculiarities that you've encountered?"

"No chocolate. Makes me retch."

Wembley's face drooped. "I mourn your loss. Vampires have no difficulty with consuming hot chocolate—dark or milk. I find both to be quite satisfying, but again, one must be mindful of the caffeine."

"What about garlic and crosses and stakes?"

"Myths, but you are as susceptible to injury as before. Increased life span and some faster healing—but stop our heart, remove our head, or break our spinal column and that's all she wrote."

"Now this is useful stuff. Anything I absolutely should not do?"

"Let common sense rule. If it hurt your human body, it's probably bad for the vamp version. Stay away from too much caffeine. Illegal drugs are usually a bad idea—although weed can be fun." I shook my head, and he smiled. "Right, no weed."

"And things I absolutely should do?"

"Keep yourself well fed—as best you can. A cranky

vamp is no one's friend." Wembley shook his head. "A few bad seeds, and we all get a bad rap."

"Alex implied that vampires weren't universally all that well liked." *Implied* seemed softer than the reality of his bald statement.

"Hmph. He can talk."

I perked up. "Hey, what exactly is Alex?"

"He gave you the thief, assassin, wizard shtick, didn't he?"

"Yes—what's all the secrecy about? I'd think what kind of..." Monster? Creature? I bit my tongue before either of those slipped out.

"Person?" Wembley gave me a wide-eyed, innocent look. Then he grinned. "Kidding aside, we're all people. Enhanced people with unique gifts, but simply people. At least, the Society members are. But as for Alex, he's most certainly a wizard. Let your freak flag fly, says I." Wembley flashed his fangs at me.

This time, it didn't startle me, and I took a closer look. Not like human teeth. The points were much sharper. Interesting.

"How is being a wizard freaky?"

Wembley sheathed his fangs before he spoke. "You're so adorably, naively cute. Like a little fluffy bunny."

"Happy is a new gig for me. I'm trying to embrace it—so don't screw with me." And then I smiled at him, because I really was embracing my happy these days.

"A little bunny with fangs—even cuter. Wizards have access to arcane, dark power. Many of the other enhanced won't mix with wizards. Although, truthfully, most of us don't commingle well. There's the born versus made divide, with each thinking the other is inferior in some way."

"Born versus made—so I'm made?"

"You are indeed so lucky—" Wembley winced. "Sorry. I keep forgetting. Accidents are so rare these days. But yes, you are made—with a tiny dash of genetic predisposition. All vamps lack a common immunity to the vampire virus. Witches are made, as well as golems, and—"

"A person made of clay?" I asked. I'd once read a legend about a creature made of clay, and I thought that had been a golem.

"Not exactly clay. More like a person created from the flesh of others. Sounds disturbing—but you've probably met a few without noticing anything different about them."

"Spiffy. Don't suppose there's any way to identify them?"

"Incredibly attractive. And there are the tattoos. They're discreetly located, so you'd have to be up close and very personal to get a look."

I tried to keep a straight face when he said it, because... yuck. Sex with someone made up of dead bits of other people. Oh, no no no.

"And the born enhanced?" I asked, trying desperately to wipe away the graphic image that had popped into my head.

"Wizards, few though they may be, assassins, and thieves all have closely related gifts and are thought to originally be from one bloodline. There's an entire religious controversy centered around the question—don't ask or you'll step on toes. We've also got a few djinn in the Austin area, and coyotes."

"Got it." I didn't have it—because coyotes?—but I would come back around to the Society members again. Other vamp things were much more pressing. "Can you do the thing with your fangs again?"

"Which thing?"

"The disappearing and reappearing fangs."

He flashed his fangs at me again. Then they disappeared. "They're retractable. Just hope they never get stuck. Speaking while fanged is a developed talent, and embarrassingly awkward in the learning stages."

"Not a problem—I don't have any."

"Hmm, no. You may have no control over them, but you certainly have them." With his thumb and forefinger, he touched the points on his mouth that mirrored the sores on my lips.

"Oh. Ooooooh." I looked around the room, didn't see a mirror, so I pulled a compact out of my purse.

"How human." Wembley seemed amused. When I looked up in confusion, he said, "Vampires don't shine, perspire, sweat—whatever you womenfolk call it these days. No need for powder—unless your skin is hideous."

I looked up from my examination of my gum line and canines.

"Not you, little fluffy bunny. You have gorgeous skin."

I couldn't remember the last time someone had given me a compliment.

"And a gorgeous smile."

"Thank you. Any reason I can't see my fangs?"

"You probably don't have a lot of control over them. Baby vamps rarely do—and you're more baby than most this long after the bite." He frowned. "And less." He scratched his chin. "You're an anomaly—so just be careful."

Be careful—of what and how? But I nodded.

"Oh, and keep an eye out for burgeoning talents."

Before I could ask about what I was on the lookout for, someone knocked at the door. Immediately thereafter, Alex entered the room. "Time to go."

I tried to stand up, but the sofa had well and truly swallowed me. "Already? I have more questions."

"It's been two and a half hours. I have a lunch date." Alex offered his hand.

"Oh—sorry. I didn't realize…" I grasped Alex's hand and he pulled me with no effort at all from the depths of the sofa. Again with the blinky light-flickering thing. I ignored it, since Alex didn't seem to notice. "Wembley, you've been so kind."

"No trouble at all. Unlike the very professional Anton, I have no card. Make sure Alex gets you my cell number. We'll do this again—soon." He raised his eyebrows and gave me an intent look.

"Yes. Absolutely. I'll be in touch."

There were so many things to talk about. The mysterious Lemann that Wembley seemed to dislike so much, what it was like being a vamp in Austin, what the Society was all about. Too many questions.

Alex was already at the door looking impatient.

"I'm coming." And I scooted quickly through the door.

We reversed our path from earlier, heading to the shop.

"Who's your date?" I asked. His face looked blank, so I clarified. "Your lunch date? A new girl or last night's girl?"

"Ah. Last night's. I should get at least a few more dates out of her."

I tried not to look judgy, but it was hard when he'd basically said he'd get a few more shags out of her and then move on. That was what it sounded like, at least. Ick. On the other hand, I *did* ask.

When we walked through the shop, the same girl was manning the register, and she didn't look like she'd moved.

In a quiet voice, I asked, "Don't the employees restock or dust when there aren't any customers?"

Alex shrugged.

"Wembley ratted you out. I know it's your store."

"That doesn't change my answer. I don't know and don't care. If the place starts to look bad, I have a word, but generally everything gets taken care of. Why nitpick? They're paid a little over minimum wage and are mostly just kids. They do a decent job, so what do I care if they occasionally play on their phones when no one's in the store?"

"Huh. That's not completely terrible reasoning." It just never would have occurred to me. I looked around the store. He was right. It was basically tidy, and while I wouldn't call it nicely merchandised, the hodgepodge mixture of items in the displays gave the place a kind of Halloween-flavored eclectic charm. "Actually, I think your lack of micro-managing might give the store some of its personality."

He gave me a knowing look then opened the door for me. He called out over his shoulder, "See you this afternoon, Mandy."

"Sure thing, Alex." The door thudded shut on the last syllable.

Alex unlocked the doors to my Jeep remotely, but he still came around and opened the door for me. The guy might be sleazy, but he could also be polite and charming.

Once he climbed in, he said, "You going to tell me what the deal with the car is? Not to dis your choice, but I'm not sure I understand the abundance of excitement you've exhibited for it."

I wrinkled my nose. He was annoyingly right. "I don't really know. Wembley thought I might have a really low-level precognition gift."

Alex barked out a laugh. "Wembley thinks everyone has a low-level precog gift. Anything less than mid-grade is hard to prove, and he's desperate for the gift to still exist."

"What, it's on the endangered gift list or something?"

"Let's just say I have my doubts about its existence. My

point is, I wouldn't put much stock in Wembley's assertions where precog is concerned." He grinned, but didn't look at me—and if I had to guess, I'd say he was laughing at me. "Did you learn anything useful?"

"That you're a wizard, and that's super spooky."

"Only to vamps." His tone was wry, so no hot buttons there. Hm. Secretive yet not ashamed.

"That some guy named Lemann is the CSO and Wembley is really suspicious of him—but no clue why."

"Sounds right."

"That there's some religious question of bloodlines and origin between the assassins, the thieves, and the wizards—but it's hush-hush and should not be mentioned for fear of pissing off the lot of you."

"Eh—that's a little last century. But it's never a bad idea to err on the side of caution with that one. But I asked if you learned anything *useful*."

"Hey—the little bits and pieces are useful when you consider I have zero context for the world I now live in." The low-grade ache of hunger in my stomach that I'd tuned out all morning was ramping up.

"Welcome to life as a Made."

My stomach cramped with hunger. "Um, I need a smoothie."

"What?"

"You're going to have to be late for you date, becuz I need uh ssake."

Alex started laughing. He tried halfheartedly to stop but then just busted out. "No problem."

I flipped down the vanity mirror. Two tiny fangs protruded from my mouth. If I wasn't careful, I'd reopen the small, almost-healed wounds on my bottom lip. So I kept my mouth very still while Alex laughed at me and my baby fangs.

It wouldn't have been quite so bad if I hadn't seen Wembley's adult version. His serpent-like fangs had been wicked. Fear inducing.

Mine were more likely to be called adorable. Little fluffy bunny, indeed.

I closed the vanity mirror with a sharp snap.

"I'm sorry—but they're so...cute." And he laughed again. "I've seen new vamp fangs before, and I never thought I'd say that. But they're so...darling." He snickered.

I sighed. A loud, very dramatic, speech-replacing sigh.

"Right. Sorry. There's a juice place just a few minutes up ahead. I was thinking you should give the mango spinach a try—decent calories and iron-rich. And"—he snickered again—"maybe you should start carrying a few spare cans of that supplement stuff that was littering your apartment when I picked you up this morning."

I didn't reply. What would I say, other than *you're right*? And that would probably come out hissy and weird with the fangs.

Finally, he drove through and snagged a mango spinach smoothie for me. I sucked on that frozen juice, tiny baby fangs hanging out for all the world to see—if they had really powerful binoculars.

About halfway through the shake, my fangs disappeared. I didn't feel them retract; they just weren't there anymore.

"You are a nasty man to kick a girl when she's down."

He gave me a sheepish look. "They're just so tiny. Like training wheel fangs."

I glared, but my heart wasn't in it. He was right. I couldn't hang on to my mad, not after having seen Wembley's grown-up version. "Uh-oh. Am I stuck with these? I mean, I don't use them to eat. Will they keep growing even though I don't drink blood?"

"Well, you're about week out from the bite?"

"Give or take, sure." Crap. Today was Tuesday. I could not forget to email work.

"I hate to tell you this, but your fangs are closer to day-old than week-old in size."

"Wizards are up to date on the transformation process of vamps?"

His body stiffened, subtly, but the change was there. "You forget; I do emergency response."

"Wembley says you're also a kind of an enforcer for the Society. Is that true?"

"It's not my job title anymore, but there's an aspect of that in what we do." He glanced at me out of the corner of his eye then back to the road. "Why?"

"Why? Because I want to know why you guys aren't hunting down the perv who bit and turned me. That's against Society regs, from what Wembley said."

"You're correct. It's highly illegal." His fingers tightened on the steering wheel. "You're not the only one."

"I'm sorry—what?"

"There have been some deaths. In order to transmit the virus, a vamp has to bite deep and drink long. The deeper the bite and longer the drink, the greater the load of the vampire virus that's delivered. And if the subject is immune and receives a large load of the virus, the body has an anaphylactic response."

"Untreated, death results," I whispered. "If I had the immunity to the virus that most people have..." I shuddered. "You guys have found the dead bodies of these other victims?"

"Not exactly. There are a few deaths that we suspect are related, all discovered through targeted research. Victims that appear to have died from untreated anaphylactic shock —all women, alone, late at night, with no known allergies. I suspect there are others we're missing. There's one case we're certain of. She sought treatment from Dr. Dobrescu, just like you did—but she didn't make it."

I clasped my arms tight around my middle and sank deeper into my seat. "What are the police doing?"

"They haven't connected the deaths, not that we know." He seemed to give his next words some serious thought. "Anton should have brought you in."

"Brought me in where?"

"To the Society."

"Isn't that basically what you're doing now? With the meeting today and everything?"

"Not exactly. You're not a member of the Society—you were a visitor today."

"Ah." I didn't actually understand the difference, but it didn't seem wise to say that.

"Membership has some small advantages. But really, if you're enhanced, you belong. The delay is a troubling reflection of some members' perception of this current crisis."

"And by crisis—you mean the murders?"

He nodded.

"I did think it was odd that no one's asking me questions. I haven't filed a report with you guys or anything. How are you even investigating?" I was feeling more and more like a victim as we spoke. A victim who wasn't looking at justice anytime soon.

"We know you went out with your friends from work on Tuesday, probably had two drinks, went home, and emerged from your apartment on Sunday in the beginnings of a transformation that should have killed you without supplemental blood feeding. Anton expected you to go home and quietly die."

That summed it up. And made my blood boil—at least, the "quietly dying" part did. "How do you know all of that?"

"Your doctor, your credit card statements, you yourself."

"And if Anton knew I was in distress, why didn't he provide specialized medical assistance? He passed that number along with instructions to call in a few days. From what you're saying, because he couldn't be bothered to deal with me and was hoping I'd croak." I could feel my heart pumping at double time. Anton was not a nice person. "Oh, and if I felt a murderous rage coming on, to phone you—that ER number. Oh. My. God. You'd have come and killed me, wouldn't you?" My eyeballs started to itch from all the air and no blinking. I blinked rapidly.

"First, what help could the Society give you? You have an aversion to blood. Only blood sustains vampires—so far as we knew till you. Second, subjects are prepared for the transformation with information, but there's no physical prep. It's a sink-or-swim process, other than providing blood. And that fits with vamp tradition: the weak die." He cracked his neck, staring straight ahead. "And I'd only kill you as a last resort."

He was kinda sleazy with his lunchtime lays, and he laughed at me when maybe he shouldn't—but I liked the guy. Besides being attractive, he was appealing in a way I couldn't quite put my finger on. And that made his words hurt.

We drove for several minutes in silence, because I didn't know what to say. I was weak. I was broken. I was expendable. No one wanted justice for me. Maybe for those other people—actually, no, not even for them. My happy was suffering several major blows. And I was hungry again. That smoothie had helped, but hadn't knocked out my hunger entirely.

He parked the Jeep in a spot near the elevator. I never got a good spot in this parking lot, and that was twice now that he'd scored a close spot. Which irritated me even more.

"Who were they?"

Alex took the keys out of the ignition and handed them to me. "Who?"

"The other victims." I didn't even try to keep the sharpness out of my voice.

"We know of three. All women, all in their mid-thirties to early forties, dark-haired, successful. And again, they all died at night, alone in their homes. You're the fourth, and fit that description, so we think it's a pattern."

And now I *felt* weak. I'd been targeted, attacked, changed —because this nut job had a thing for my type. No one had before, and it just figured that when someone did, it would be all about pervy needs and murder.

"Except I didn't die."

He was completely still in the driver's seat. You don't notice the small movements people make, until they freeze completely. Then the motionlessness is eerie and the lack of movement noticeable. Finally, he said, "No. You didn't die."

It had been freeing to be rid of the anxieties that, in retrospect, I'd clearly been living with for a long time. But that freedom, the joy of it, was fading. There was a killer out there. He'd violated me. Killed me—my human self, anyway. Completely ended the lives of at least three other women. And he was footloose and fancy-free.

"Your eyes are glowing."

I whipped my head around and stared at him. "Yeah? Is that a problem?"

Alex sighed. "Get it under control before you run into anyone. Hang on." He got out of my car, pulled out his own keys, and unlocked a Honda Accord parked a few spots away. He rummaged around in the center console and emerged with a pair of sunglasses. "Here."

I'd followed him to his car, and now took the tinted glasses. I put them on without a word, and turned on my heel. I had things to do—like catch a killer.

Then I spoiled my fabulous exit, because I realized that I needed those names. I stopped, turned, and said, "Text me their names."

He didn't ask who; he just nodded.

And then I turned on my heel for the second time and marched away.

10

FAREWELL, MRS. ARBUTHNOT

F ired up and on a mission, I didn't notice all of the noise when I first got off the elevator on the fourth floor. But I could hardly miss the hubbub once I turned the corner. I backed away, hoping no one had seen me. As quickly as I could, I tucked away the sunglasses Alex had loaned me and pulled out my compact. My eyes looked just fine. A little more bloodshot than usual, maybe, but the pupils were a normal size and the irises the same shade of blue they'd always been.

I took a breath to steady my nerves and turned the corner again.

Sally, whose last name I'd never known and who lived a few doors down, was in the hall talking to old Mr. Simms. And the shut-in from the end of the hall whose first name I couldn't recall at the moment was standing a few feet away from the other two, listening and looking forlorn.

Another group had formed, but they were all from the other side of the floor—so I really didn't know them at all.

Where was the perpetually nosy Mrs. A? Her absence was the equivalent of the news failing to report a presidential election's results—or roughly that. She was *the* floor busybody.

I approached Sally, Mr. Simms, and unknown shut-in guy. "Where is Mrs. A?"

But I knew as soon as the words left my lips—this hallway gathering, this hubbub, it was about her.

Sally looked at me like I was an alien from another planet, but Mr. Simms replied. "Hi, Mallory. There's some bad news. Mrs. A was found a little earlier in her apartment. It looks like maybe a suicide."

"No. That's not right. Mrs. A would never do that." And I knew I was right. Like I knew that I wanted that Grand Cherokee, and I knew I wanted to live in a place like that quiet south Austin neighborhood. No way did Mrs. A kill herself. The woman was vibrant. She embraced every day, was mindful of her health, ate well, exercised. No way.

"I know it's shocking, but that's the way it's looking. Pills..." Mr. Simms cast his eyes downward. He lived alone—most of us on this floor did because they were all one-bedrooms—but he didn't get out a lot. Mrs. A, with her busybody ways, was probably one of his few social outlets.

I hugged him.

What could I say? The guy looked like he needed a hug. And he hugged me back, so I was probably right.

"Who are you?" Sally asked.

"Mallory Andrews." I let go of Mr. Simms and pointed to my apartment door. We'd definitely been introduced at least three times. And had run into each other innumerable times in the hallway and elevator.

"That was sort of rhetorical." Sally eyed me from head to toe. "You look different, dress different, and act different. It's that new guy you're dating, isn't it?"

Was she channeling my mother?

Then I remembered. "Ah, you chatted with Mrs. A. I think she misunderstood..." But I realized suddenly that Mrs. A might have misunderstood, but it didn't matter. Not at all. Because Mrs. A was dead. My breath caught in my chest.

"She told me all about the man you came home with the other night." Sally spoke in low tones, giving Mrs. A some deference—but Sally was all about the gossip. Which actually made it easier to breathe. Mrs. A had been all about the gossip, too.

Mr. Simms shook his head and walked away. I liked to think it was Sally's poor taste and not the false information about me bringing a man home that had him on the run.

But then shut-in guy stepped up. "Bradley," he said.

From that awkward interjection, I gathered that was both his name and an attempt to introduce himself.

I held out my hand. "Hello, Bradley. I'm—"

"Mallory Andrews. I know." He seemed to give the decision as to whether to shake my hand or not serious consideration, then grabbed it, pumped it once, and let go.

Awkward pretty much summed him up.

"Did you know Mrs. A?" I asked.

"Arbuthnot. Mrs. Arbuthnot liked it that I called her by her real last name and not Mrs. A. She said you brought a date home on Tuesday night, and that he was 'good-looking enough for that type.' But she didn't say what type, and I don't know what that means, really. But she seemed happy for you."

My eyes teared up. Or they tried to. They ended up kinda burning and itching more than anything. I knew she didn't approve of my single state. And that she could be judgmental about certain other things—my weight, for one —but she'd been a kind woman. And she had been nosy because she cared about her neighbors. Why did she have to care about me and then go and die?

I rubbed my eyes, but that only made them burn more.

Sally looked at me uncertainly. "Do you need a hanky or something?"

I was about to decline, but a nasty thought occurred. "Wait a minute. I really don't have a boyfriend." I turned to Bradley. "Are you sure she said Tuesday?"

Bradley nodded. "I'm good with the little things. Mrs. Arbuthnot liked that. I remembered her birthday and that she liked irises. They're a showy flower, but she liked them all the same. That's what she used to say. So I bought her irises for her birthday every year."

I looked at Bradley with new eyes. "How long have you lived here, Bradley?"

"Eight years, just like Mrs. Arbuthnot. She moved in when her husband passed, because what better way to stay young than to live in the center of all the excitement. She used to say that."

"I'd forgotten that." Sally smiled sadly. "I heard her say that."

I felt a burn again, but this time it was in my gut—and for the first time since my change, it wasn't hunger. "No way she killed herself."

I couldn't say anything to these completely non-paranormal or occult-involved people, but I'd bet Mrs. A saw the vile thing who'd bit me. And he was apparently "good-looking enough for that type." My scalp crawled.

"I think you're right." Bradley pulled a key out of his pocket. "I have a key to her apartment, and she said I could use it if ever there was an emergency. This is an emergency." Bradley blinked owlishly at me.

"Bradley, I'd hug you, but I don't think you'd like it much, would you?"

"No. Thank you." He shifted from foot to foot. "So you'll help look inside her apartment? To see why the paramedics think she hurt herself? Because that's not right. Mrs. Arbuthnot wouldn't do that. She promised to bring me chicken soup tomorrow."

"Whoa. Stop now," Sally said. "I'm on the homeowners' association board, so I'm just going to disappear and pretend I didn't hear any of that." She reached out and squeezed Bradley's shoulder. "But good luck." Then she vanished in a cloud of expensive perfume.

"I like Sally. She always smells nice."

"Yeah, Bradley, I guess she does." I glanced down the hall to see if the other group had dispersed, and it looked like they were making motions in that direction. Just another minute or two.

"You were a little mean before. You're nicer now."

I turned back to look at him. I didn't remember ever actually speaking to him. "I'm really sorry about that."

"That's okay. If you can fix this, I forgive you."

But no one could fix this. Mrs. A was dead, probably murdered by the crazy man who'd bitten me.

"I'll do whatever I can, Bradley. You have my word."

And I would—even if that involved breaking and entering.

11

NOT BREAKING, DEFINITELY ENTERING

I took the key Bradley had given me and opened Mrs. A's door. Bradley followed close behind and quietly pulled the door shut.

I'd been in her condo several times. She liked to stay involved with the condo community, and as a result, she hosted the occasional floor social and a monthly bridge night—but that was more appealing to the older crowd and a few couples in their twenties. But I was one of the few who received private invitations. She'd sometimes have me over for a glass of wine and a chat.

Her condo looked as it always did, with one notable exception: the bathroom. Pills were scattered on the tile floor and one towel was askew on the rack, with the other piled on the floor. It looked like she might have grabbed at the towels or the bar where they hung as she'd fallen.

Bradley came up behind me and looked over my shoulder into the bathroom.

"Who takes a bunch of pills and stands around waiting for them to take effect?" I asked.

"Who takes pills without a drink?" Bradley replied. "I always drink a full glass of water."

"You might be unique in that, Bradley. Most of us don't follow the directions on the bottle. But I do think most people take pills with water or some kind of drink. Especially if you're taking a lot of pills. Go check the kitchen for glass in the sink."

I already knew from a quick visual inspection on entering that there wasn't anything on the counters.

"That's silly. She wouldn't take the pills in the kitchen and then come back to the bathroom and spill more pills."

"We absolutely agree on that." I looked over my shoulder to give him an encouraging smile. "Go check real quick. I'll see what it is that she supposedly took."

After he left, I entered the bathroom, careful not to step on the handful of scattered pills. In the corner was a pill bottle. I'd have thought paramedics would have grabbed that for purposes of determining what she'd taken and treating the overdose. But if she'd been dead when they arrived...?

I grabbed a bit of tissue and used it to turn the bottle so I could read the name: hydrocodone. And the prescription was for Mrs. A. An older one, but it was hers. Then I put the bottle back as it had been.

I stepped out of the bathroom to find Bradley waiting.

"No glass in the sink, and the dishwasher was empty. Mrs. Arbuthnot was always tidy. And she was a lady—she wouldn't drink straight from the tap or out of her hand."

"Agreed." I checked my phone for overdose with hydrocodone. I scanned the contents. Then turned the screen so Bradley could read it. "I don't know. Seems like you'd go lie down, right? Slowed breathing, low blood pressure, drowsiness. If she did this to herself—" I held up my hand when Bradley started to protest. "I don't think she did. I'm just hypothesizing. If she did, she'd go lie down in her bedroom."

We shared a glance and then Bradley took off at a trot for her bedroom.

I arrived just a few seconds after him. He was staring at the tidily made bed, shaking his head. "This is all wrong. Why would someone hurt her?"

"Because people suck." I walked closer to the bed and squatted so I was at eye level. Not a dimple in the thin coverlet. No one had lain on this bed since it had been made.

Bradley looked lost, and he kept saying, "It's all wrong. Just wrong."

I wasn't sure what I'd do if the guy started crying. I wasn't really equipped to deal with awkward, introverted, crying people.

"Come on. Let's get out of here. We've seen what we need to see." When Bradley hesitated, I said, "How about a cup of tea?"

He eyed me speculatively. "Okay, but at my place. I don't know about your tea."

I tried not to laugh, because laughter would be beyond inappropriate in the situation. But his suspicion of my tea products was just a little bit funny. I was a *vampire*. And I wanted to laugh. I really didn't want to cry. If I even *could* cry.

I looked around one last time, and then turned to Bradley and said, "Deal. Besides, my place is a bit of a mess right now. I'm thinking about moving, so I'm packing."

"Don't normal people find a place first and then pack?"

And then I did let myself smile. "You're assuming I'm normal. I don't think I am."

I pulled out my phone and looked for the series of

missed calls from the morning. Bingo. I had Alex's number. I knew it; his personal cell was different from the emergency response number I'd dialed the day before.

Once we were out in the hall, I locked up and returned the key to Bradley. Then I texted Alex: *Neighbor likely witness. Found dead, 911 suspect suicide. I think murdered.*

After I hit send, I followed Bradley down the hall to his place. I had a thought: maybe it was Bradley? And he was luring me into his den to finish me off.

Cue the creepy music now.

No. No way. No way in this lifetime or the next five lifetimes.

First, that was crazy.

Second, Bradley had lived in the building for eight years, per him. But I knew for sure it was at least five years, because he'd been here when I bought my place. Which made me cringe that I couldn't remember the guy's name earlier.

And second, just no way.

And third, he really seemed to care about Mrs. A.

So I trotted—hopped?—behind him like the naïve bunny Wembley had claimed I was, and I didn't worry about him turning ninja killer on me.

When I walked into his condo, I did a double take. Pottery Barn? Not the look I would have guessed. I'd have thought IKEA meets Star Trek would have been closer.

Bradley gave me an impatient look. "The kitchen is this way."

Which I knew, of course, because there were only a few one-bedroom floor plans.

"I was just admiring your living room."

Bradley nodded. "Thank you. Mrs. Arbuthnot helped me decorate. She said that a comfortable home was important if I wanted to date." He narrowed his eyes at me and said, "I don't want to date."

I swallowed a smile. Since the thought hadn't—and never would—cross my mind, it was a little funny rather than offensive that Bradley felt the need to proactively ward off my advances. "I bet you never told her that."

"No. She thought everyone should get married. I didn't want to disappoint her." Bradley looked around his apartment. "And I like this much better than before."

"You were really close, weren't you?" Mrs. A had touched a lot of lives. If I wasn't careful, I'd get all almost-teary again.

Bradley nodded and then walked into the kitchen.

I looked around one more time, looking for some clue as to what exactly Bradley did in here all day, but it didn't look like his living room was where he worked. When I walked into the kitchen, I remembered this particular plan had a small office that was an offshoot of the bedroom. That was likely where Bradley's highly segmented work life lived. He seemed a guy for categories and tidiness of all varieties.

He'd already put a kettle on to boil when I joined him.

"I have that one; it sings."

"I don't like the loud noises the other kind make."

I sat down at the kitchen table. "I don't suppose you would. What kind of tea do you have?"

"I have chamomile, peppermint, and Scottish breakfast. The Scottish breakfast was for Mrs. Arbuthnot."

"Ah. Would you like to drink that one in her honor? Or save it?"

Bradley seemed to give my question great consideration. Then he retrieved milk from the refrigerator. "Mrs. Arbuthnot drinks it...drank it with milk."

"Well, that's exactly how we'll drink it, then, isn't it?"

"Mrs. Arbuthnot has a fancy cream pitcher she'd put the

milk in when I would have tea in her home. But this is what we did here." He retrieved some very pretty teacups and saucers and placed them on the table. "Another important clue: Mrs. Arbuthnot didn't like taking those pills. They were for her arthritis, but she said they made her head all foggy and made her want to sleep more."

"Right. Mrs. A wouldn't like anything that slowed her down. She swore that walking kept her arthritis in check."

He nodded. "She took over-the-counter drugs, mostly."

The kettle began to sing, and Bradley turned it off immediately. He poured loose tea in to a teapot that matched the delicate cups he'd placed on the table. Mrs. A really had influenced him. I couldn't help wonder if she'd been his best friend. Maybe his only real friend.

"Bradley, can you tell more about the man who came home with me on Tuesday?"

He gave me an odd look. "He was with *you*. You know about him."

"Just humor me."

He placed the pot on the table. "We have to let it steep now. Does this have something to do with Mrs. Arbuthnot's murder?"

"It might. That man who was with me—he was..." I hadn't quite thought that through. "I didn't invite him."

He peered at me. "You can't remember."

I licked my lips, and realized I was quite thirsty. "No."

"Did he hurt you?"

My brain was thinking "yes," but my mouth said, "No." He hadn't actually hurt me—unless I died in the next few days from starvation, but that was looking less and less likely. "In the end, it turned out he didn't hurt me, but he tried to."

"I'm sorry. That shouldn't have happened."

And then I really did cry. No one had said sorry. No one had expressed an iota of sympathy or regret on my behalf. Not my doctor, certainly not Anton, and Alex and Wembley, though somewhat more helpful, hadn't ever extended any specific expressions of sympathy. The socially awkward shut-in was the first person to say the right thing. My throat closed with unshed tears.

My eyes were burning now, like they had before, but I could feel the moisture gathering in my eyes.

And then the first tear slipped down my face.

"Ow." It stung. A lot. It was an itchy, burning sting. I hopped up, lifted a finger, grabbed my bag, and ran to the bathroom.

I splashed water on face several times, but after several attempts there was still a mild sting. It felt like the time I'd been out wade-fishing in the bay with my dad and the water had been filled with jellyfish. The water had been so full of them that it had carried a hint of the translucent spawn of Satan's poison. And then one of them had wrapped its tentacled self around my bare calf. My scalp crawled thinking about it. I still hated those nasty see-through critters.

I flushed my eyes out some more and then alternated between flushing my eyes and splashing my face. When I'd done as much as I could, I grabbed a towel and patted my face dry.

Peering at the mirror, I was more than a little surprised to find faint burn marks running down my face. I'd just burned myself—with my own tears. Chalk that one up to weird vampire things no one thinks to tell you about.

With a sense of smug self-satisfaction, I took out my powder compact—the one that no vampire would need, per Wembley—and evened out my skin.

It didn't take much to cover the marks, but if I'd come

out of the bathroom with pink streaks down my face, even Bradley might have been suspicious.

When I joined Bradley at the kitchen table, he'd already poured tea for both of us. I sat down, apologizing.

"No problem. Milk, like Mrs. Arbuthnot?"

A nodded firmly. "Absolutely." But I poured it myself and just barely added any. Milk was on my "do-not-consume" list.

We drank in silence for some time. I'd finished my cup and was well into my second when Bradley said, "She just said he was good-looking enough for that type."

"Yes, you said that earlier. Do you know what type she meant?"

He shook his head. "She didn't say."

"And you didn't see anything?"

"No, it was after dinner. I work after dinner."

My ears perked up. "What do you do?"

"I build apps. I'm good with details."

I supposed that made sense. Writing code—if that was in fact what he was doing—did require an eye for detail. "Do you remember anything else that Mrs. A said about the man?"

"He must have gone in with you and stayed a long time, because Mrs. Arbuthnot didn't see him leave, and she stays up late. Insomnia."

My skin crawled. What had he been doing in my apartment all that time?

Drinking my blood? Watching TV? Digging through my underwear drawer?

Ick. Ick, icky, ick.

Bradley poured more tea for both of us. "I'll have to make another pot, if you want more."

"No, thank you." What I really needed was a gallon of water and some vegan nutrition supplement shakes.

My phone rang, cutting short my train of thought. Good thing. I didn't need my fangs poking out inopportunely.

A local number came up on the caller ID. "Hello?"

"Where are you? I'm knocking on your door, and you're not answering." Alex sounded annoyed that his unexpected visit had been derailed.

I rolled my eyes. "I'm not in my condo. I'm down the hall; not that it's any business of yours. I just texted. Proper etiquette is to text a reply."

"You're okay?"

"Perfectly safe, right down the hall." I sighed. I did need his help. "Be right there."

I finished my tea with one very unladylike gulp, and sent my apologies up to Mrs. A. She would not have approved.

"Thank you, Bradley. I've got someone waiting who can help with the case. Or at least will believe it wasn't suicide or an accident." I stood up, but then paused to add, "You'll let me know if you think of anything to do with the man on Tuesday or Mrs. A's death?"

"Yes."

Then I remembered that I'd probably be moving soon. So I left him with my cell number, in case I wasn't home or had started to move.

He walked with me to the door and opened it for me.

"Thank you," I said. "Mrs. A was lucky to have you for friend."

Bradley looked positively lost at my words. I kissed him on the cheek and booked it down the hallway before he could utter a word.

12

VAMPIRE TEARS AND CROCODILE SMILES

Alex could make what he would of me running down the hallway like a crazy woman. His good opinion wasn't high on my priority list. His help, however...

I put my hands on my hips. "Why didn't you just let yourself in?"

He gave me a one-shouldered shrug. "I hear it's in bad taste."

I pulled my keys from my purse and unlocked the door. Waving him inside, I said, "You've been inside already, haven't you? Don't answer that." I walked into the kitchen, leaving him to follow or not. I needed some chow, and fast. My baby fangs were staying right where they belonged —hidden.

I popped the top on the shake I'd retrieved from the fridge.

"So exactly how good are you with security? Modern security?"

Alex strolled into the kitchen. "Why?"

"Our bad guy delivered me to the house and hung out in

CATE LAWLEY

my condo for a few hours Tuesday evening. Mrs. A—" I had to stop and take a breath, because my eyes were burning suspiciously again. Once I was sure my face wasn't in danger of scalding, I said, "Mrs. A was killed because she saw him— I'm sure of it. I wouldn't have a clue, but she happens to be the floor's managing Mary, so she told everyone I have a new man."

"One presumes there is no man, so..."

"Right. So that's the guy. She saw someone escort me home, come in with me, and not leave until after she'd gone to bed. She hinted at my having an overnight gentleman caller when I saw her...I think on Saturday?" All the days were running together. And with all of the blacking out and no work... "Nuts! I need to send my resignation email."

"Now?"

Since I was opening up my laptop and sitting down at the kitchen table in front of it, it didn't take a genius to see that I was doing it now. "Give me a break. It'll take two seconds."

In fact, it took about a minute and a half. It was shockingly easy to say: *I quit, and put me in touch with HR so I can fill out the right paperwork.* Boom. Done. Again, the feeling of a load lifting lightened me. If I got any lighter from all of my burden shedding, I'd be able to fly.

"Vampires can't fly, can they?"

Alex looked at me like I'd grown five heads.

"I'll take that as a no. Security—so you have wicked stealth skills, yes?"

Alex dropped down into a chair kitty-corner from me. "What's Wembley been saying?"

"Not much at all. No, you seem to have a knack for evading security, and since there's that whole thief/assassin connection, I thought you might have useful skills."

"Just tell me already. What do you want?"

"I *need* the security video from the parking garage on Tuesday evening. And if there's video in the elevator, that too."

"Easy enough."

"You can do it?" I almost clapped my hands, but I stopped myself just in time. All of this burden-lightening and happy-embracing was turning me into a giddy cheerleader.

"Easy enough to give you an answer. Most vamps can mask themselves on electronic recording devices."

"For reals? That is handy." I could venture forth in true anonymity. Simultaneously disturbing and liberating. "Wait, he'd have to know he was being recorded. We should check —can you get it?"

"I already have it, and I've already checked. There's nothing useful for purposes of ID."

I narrowed my eyes and gave him the third-degree look. "That sounded like legal speak. What *is* on that footage?"

"You. Looking drunk and coming home alone."

"But that's not right. There was a guy who brought me home on Tuesday—or at least to my door."

"I'm sure there was." He managed to sound mostly genuine and only a little condescending.

I'd finished my shake and could use another dozen or so. After I retrieved a six-pack, I sat back down. "Why are you here?"

"The murder of your neighbor was unexpected. It doesn't fit the pattern. And..." A scowl fell over his face.

"You were worried about me."

He met my gaze briefly. "You're the first survivor. That we know of, anyway."

"But I'm not a witness."

"You're certain of that?"

I ignored the question and popped open another shake. Straws; I needed to buy straws. Was I a witness? Ugh—I couldn't even go there now. Surely I'd been unconscious. "Since I don't do blood—and clearly I've never bitten anyone—what's the procedure?"

"Fangs extend, puncture, drink, apply pressure, lick to seal, and done."

"You're telling me my spit seals wounds?"

"No. I'm telling you the saliva from a vamp who has just consumed blood *heals* small wounds. And leaves no scars, unless you pierce the same location over and over."

"That is so disgusting." But fascinating. And handy info to have. "So if I could eat blood, I could heal small wounds."

"But you can't."

"But if I could... You're right; it doesn't matter. But how do they—the blood-drinking part of the population—find people to suck on? Volunteers? Mind control? And do the victims remember?"

Alex sighed. "I'm assuming you'll be more careful with your language when you meet other vampires—" I inhaled to speak, but he shushed me. "I've made an appointment for you to meet the Society's CSO on Friday. There's no mind control—subtle persuasion, but that's not even remotely like mind control. Mind control is taboo. That means not allowed. Very bad."

"I get it." Not like I could control anyone's mind. Someone was a little touchy on the mind control thing.

"Most vamps don't risk live biting any more. Remember, I told you there's bottled blood at the Society's headquarters."

"Ick. Wouldn't it be all clotted and thick and nasty once you stored it?"

"There are certain natural anti-coagulants that enhance the flavor. There are also witch-crafted stasis bottles that keep blood fresh for weeks, sometimes months."

I blinked. "Stasis. Wow. But we digress. The real question is how did my blood get sucked, and I don't remember anything?"

"I'm thinking you were roofied."

My jaw dropped. That had never occurred to me. I didn't know why. "Is there some witch brew or special magical concoction that impacts memory?"

"Ever heard of Rohypnol? The sedative?"

"Oh, literally roofied." I got a tight, panicky feeling in my chest. "If he drank a bunch of my blood, and I couldn't tell, do you think—"

"No." He snapped the word out. His tone softer, he said, "You'd know. Vamps heal faster than humans, but you would know." He caught my panicky gaze. "You would know."

I chugged the shake, tried to not think too much about how vulnerable I'd been, and chugged some more. "Can I still get drunk?"

"Normal vamps can. Takes a little more—but sure. Feeling the need for a drink?"

I got up and dug around in the very back of my pantry. I thought I had— "Ha! There it is." I came back to the table brandishing a bottle of Johnnie Walker Black Label. "I don't normally do scotch, but it's what we've got. Join me?"

He nodded, so I retrieved two glasses.

Alex poured. He lifted his glass and said, "To new beginnings."

"Heck yes. New beginnings." I lifted my glass and saluted him.

I was about to find out if my new virus-laden body could

stomach booze. I threw back the entire contents of the glass. It burned a little, not so much as I remembered, then it spread through my body with a nice, rosy glow.

I set the glass back on the table and considered the state of my stomach. "The new me might like scotch."

Alex poured me another.

"So, back to being a witness...on Tuesday, I went to work, I had drinks with my horrible coworkers, and that's all I remember."

"How'd you get home?"

"No clue."

"What time did you leave the bar?"

"Ah." I got a little excited. "I left work at six thirty and met up with Liz, Penelope, Shelley, and Martin."

"What was that? That face?"

"It's Martin. He's a complete reptile." I almost laughed when I remembered. "I had this image of him bursting out of an eggshell, fully formed, with this slimy smile. Ugh. He makes my skin crawl with his shiny veneer stretched over his absolutely rotten innards." I took a sip of scotch. "Sorry, I've just never liked him, and he's always been particularly nasty to me."

"No problem. He sounds thoroughly unlikable." Alex cupped his glass, but he'd barely touched his scotch.

"I've never seen him eat. What do you think? Vamp?"

"You think that's a possibility?" He abandoned his scotch to pull out his cell. "What's his last name?" When I gave him a curious look and didn't answer, he said, "I'm just checking on his status. I'm not going to have him murdered in his bed."

Funny that Alex's brain went immediately to stealthy murder. I really needed to get the scoop on what wizards could do—and assassins and thieves. "Shade. Martin Shade."

Alex tapped out a text and sent it. He looked up and asked, "Anything else you can remember from that night?"

"That they're all ungrateful so-and-sos. I always picked up the tab when we went out." I swallowed a big gulp of scotch. After the burn had died away, I said, "I had some half-baked desire to fit in. Just enough to pick up the tab and go out every time they asked, but not enough to try very hard to be nice." I shook my head. "Don't ask. I was a different person."

"A week ago?"

"Hey, this transformation thing did something—I don't know what, but it's been a blessing. In retrospect, I probably should have taken the antianxiety drugs my cranky-old-guy doctor tried to prescribe. But I didn't, and, as a result, maybe made my life a little more difficult than it needed to be."

"Or you're hypercritical of yourself, like a lot of modern women."

I finished off my drink as I considered exactly what "modern women" might mean. "How old are you?

"Older than you."

"Huh. Okay, if that's the way you're going to be. How long do vamps typically live?"

"That number varies wildly, so I'd hardly say there's a typical." I gave him a hard look, which resulted in small huff of annoyance, but then he added, "I'd say chances for a lengthy life greatly increase if you can survive the first three to five years."

I stopped halfway through slamming my third shake of the afternoon. "There's a high mortality rate for baby vamps."

"Well, technically a baby vamp is what we call you guys

as you go through the transformation. Three to five years is just young."

I'd heard about all I could absorb on vamp lore for one day. The tiny synapses in my brain seemed to be struggling to keep up. I chugged the second half of my shake. Or I was too hungry to think straight. But I did have one more question. "What's the deal with vampire tears?"

"A myth? Vampires don't cry. Why do you ask?"

"Never mind." I'd ask Wembley next time I saw him, because it looked like I'd found a gap in Alex's knowledge.

"I think your phone's ringing."

"Huh?" But then I heard the faint buzz. I must have turned the volume down by accident. When I picked it up, I saw I had ten missed texts and four missed calls, all from work. I pointed at the phone. "Do you mind?"

Alex shook his head, grabbed his drink, and moved into the living room.

I steeled myself for a very unpleasant conversation, and answered the phone.

13

SILENT CORPSE, CHATTY SPIRITS

I hung up the phone and went hunting for Alex. I'd need him for this.

He was lounging on the sofa in my living room texting. He'd found the one piece of furniture I was definitely bringing with me to the new house—whenever I got around to moving.

I grabbed Alex's arm and hauled him to his feet. "I need you."

"Yes, mistress."

Once he was on his feet, I grabbed my purse and keys. "Seriously—I'm not kidding. That was my office. Liz hasn't been in to work for few days now, and she hasn't called in. Something's wrong."

"Liz from Tuesday night?" When I nodded, his demeanor changed. "Give me the keys—I'm driving. And go grab a few of those shakes. We don't how long we'll be gone."

"Good call." I ran into the kitchen and picked up the last three cans. I'd have to make a pit stop for supplies at some point.

Alex stood with the door open, waiting. "Do you have the address?"

"I know where it is. She hosted the last Christmas party."

"Nine months ago? Really?"

"It's pretty easy to find."

Fifteen minutes later, Alex said, "Easy to find, huh?"

"It's one of these three streets. And I know exactly what the house looks like. It's impossible to miss. It's this unusual pinky-tan color."

"Like that one up on the right?"

"Yes! That's it. And you're sure you can get us inside?"

"I've said I could three times now. Ask again and I'm locking you in the car."

I looked at the lock on the passenger door. "The locks don't work that way. You can't do that."

He lifted an eyebrow.

Nuts. I bit my tongue.

Alex parked in the drive. There wasn't a car visible, but Liz's Mini was probably in the garage. It was that kind of neighborhood.

He pulled the keys out of the ignition and looked at me. "All right. You get out, walk up to the front door as if you're going straight in. No looking about or lurking."

"And then what?"

"Then we go inside."

He got out of the car and started up the walkway.

I slid out of the Jeep as quickly as I could while trying to look as normal as possible.

By the time I got to the front door, Alex had opened it and then pulled it almost shut again. "Go back and wait in the car."

"No. That wasn't the deal."

Alex scanned the surrounding area. As far as passersby

could see, we were having a conversation. "The deal's changed. Get back in the car."

The little bit of happy that I'd been so desperately clinging to the last few days had deflated with Mrs. A's death, and now it took another hit. "She's dead."

Alex's face tightened, which was all the answer I needed. "You don't need to go inside."

I took a breath and shoved past him. Because I did need to.

She wasn't my friend, but I'd known her. More than Alex could say. We'd worked together for years. And on some level, Alex must have agreed. Because as stern as his command to retreat had been, he let me pass.

I noticed the smell first. Decay. Not overpowering, but a hint of it in the air. That must have been what had tipped off Alex. I checked the bedroom first. It seemed the logical choice.

When I went to open the door, Alex was there first. He blocked the doorway with his body and held up a finger. "Give me just a second."

I nodded. I was terrified of what I'd find on the other side of that door, so I was happy to let someone else take that first step.

He walked through the door, and no more than a minute or two later came back out. "It looks like anaphylaxis, just like the other women."

I nodded.

"You don't have to go in." Alex still stood between me and the dead body of my coworker. "There's no unseeing this."

"I understand." I put my hand on the doorknob, and he moved out of the way.

Like the rest of the house, everything was sparklingly

clean, but there was an air of untidiness—a crumpled dress thrown atop the armchair in the corner, a pair of high heels kicked off in the corner, and a pile of mail on the dresser. She likely had an exceptional cleaning lady but couldn't quite keep up the house in between visits. That sounded a lot like Liz.

My eyes had skittered past the bed, where a vaguely human shape lay—but now I let myself look.

Alex must have tidied the sheets, because they were tucked modestly around her body. I stepped closer. Her face and neck were covered in a bright red rash. The pinkish red hue of the rash clashed horribly with the mass of fiery orange-red hair strewn across her pillow. Her eyes were swollen shut. She had furrows scratched into her neck and above her clavicles. Her milky skin stained with a rash and covered in wounds was a grotesque sight. Her hands were tucked under the sheets, but I'd bet she'd have dried blood on them. I leaned in—and saw the bluish tint of her lips and the skin around them.

A touch at my shoulder made me jump.

"Come on," Alex said. "I made a call, so it won't be much longer before the police come by to check on the tip."

I nodded, half hearing him. Then his words fully registered and I turned my back on the bed, on the body, and walked away. "We need to see if there's evidence of him in the house."

"Where? This place is pretty tidy. And it doesn't look like she's invited anyone over for drinks or dinner. And she didn't have sex in that bed."

I really didn't want to know how he knew that.

I scanned the room, looking for anything, even a hint, that a man had been there. "Wait a sec." I walked over to the dresser and flipped through the mail there. It was at least a week's worth, probably more like two. I pulled out the credit card bill and bank statements from the pile. "What about these? Any chance we can see how she spent her money in the last few days before she died?"

Alex snatched them from my hand. "Possibly. Let's go."

As I walked out, her body exerted a kind of pressure on me, and I couldn't stop myself from looking over my shoulder. I was far enough away that I couldn't see the details—and my mind replaced the missing information with a picture of Liz as she had been. "She was beautiful."

"I'm sure."

"No, I mean really gorgeous." I pulled my eyes away from the bed. "No plastic surgery or sophisticated makeup —just bone-deep beautiful. You can't see that the way she is now. How she looked, it was so much a part of who she was." An exasperated sigh escaped my lips. "She always picked the wrong men. Married, mean, abusers, users..."

"Come on."

"Right—did you check the kitchen?"

"He wasn't in the kitchen. The front hallway and the bedroom, not the kitchen or anywhere else."

"How do you know that? Are you part bloodhound or something?" I stopped in the hallway, in front of the main door. "You're not part werewolf, are you?"

"Werewolves? You are kidding, right?"

"That's a no, then?"

Alex opened the door and nudged me over the threshold. "Maybe an angry witch transformed an ex into a snake or a frog at some point in the distant past. But there's no such thing as werewolves." He pulled the door shut, almost on my toes.

I hopped back. "Tell me you're kidding. Or exaggerating." Outside of my fear of snakes, that was wrong on a basic human level.

Alex shrugged and then he placed two fingers—not the pads, but the backs—lightly against the keyhole. A tiny click followed.

"Let's go."

"How...?"

When he saw I wasn't following him, he said, "It's called whispering or loosening, depending on how you do it. It's something most wizards and thieves master at a young age. Let's go."

I trotted out to the car and slid into the passenger seat. But once inside, I couldn't help thinking we'd missed something. "How do you know he was only in the hallway and the bedroom?"

"One of my spirit guides told me." Alex's facetious tone put my hackles up.

"Come on. Liz may not have been a friend, but I've known her for years. You could at least try to take this seriously."

We were only about a block and a half away, but Alex whipped the car into a curbside parking spot and turned to me with a nasty cast to his face. "I take my craft very seriously. It is a very personal—no, a *private* endeavor. Your questions are invasive and insensitive. So next time listen more closely and take a hint." Then he pointed to the approaching police car. "When I say that we need to leave..."

Nuts. A few seconds longer and that cop could have caught us in the house.

"When you say it, you mean it. Got it, and I'm sorry." And I was. I *should* have listened, but he could be a little less prickly.

He didn't say a word, just pulled back out into the street.

Belatedly, I remembered what Wembley had said about wizards and arcane, dark powers. Maybe working with Alex hadn't been my best idea.

I rode silently next to him for several miles. I wasn't sure where we were headed, but he'd just passed the exit for my condo.

Finally, when I couldn't stand the silence any longer, I said, "Am I allowed to ask why you always drive, even when we take my car?"

Some of the tension eased from his shoulders. "Sure. I'm a control freak. It gives me a panic attack to ride in the passenger seat."

And there was that facetious tone again...but this time I really listened. And what I heard was: it made him uncomfortable. Flip, but with an underpinning of truth.

So when he said his spirit guides had told him where the murdering rat had been... "You talk to the dead." It popped out of my mouth all its own. I gasped and wished the seat would swallow me whole. "Ohmygosh. I'm so sorry. Forget I said that."

"You're a walking catastrophe."

"I swear I wasn't like this before. It's like all my filters are gone. I'm sure I'll get better. Right?" I looked at him, then realized asking for reassurance from the guy I'd probably deeply offended was a less-than-clever idea. "But again— I'm so sorry. Forget I said anything."

"If you do happen to stumble upon another wizard, just don't speak. Most of them aren't as mellow as me."

I bit my lip.

He glanced at me out of the corner of his eye and then laughed. He even sounded a little amused. "Trust me; those guys make me look like the social chair of a frat."

"Really?"

"You're a complete menace. Make an effort to think first *then* speak when you meet Cornelius. Or better yet, just listen."

"Uh, who's Cornelius, and when am I meeting him?"

"Cornelius Lemann is the CSO of the Society, and you're meeting him in about five minutes."

Sure enough, we were pulling off the freeway only minutes away from the Society's headquarters.

14

PARANOIA AND THE INQUISITION

He wasn't what I expected. Chief security officer sounded so large and important. As Mrs. A would have said, "showy."

Cornelius Lemann was not showy. He was only a few inches taller than me, and he was quiet. Not his voice—his presence. He exuded a quiet confidence, an utterly believable competence. He had a neatly trimmed salt-and-pepper beard that seemed to emphasize his piercing blue eyes. And a slight British accent when he spoke—though his conversation seemed as American as my own.

Alex had whisked me through the shop and back into a far corner of the warehouse, where Cornelius's office was located.

Upon the introductions, he'd insisted I call him Cornelius, even though I suspected Wembley's use of his last name was more typical.

I liked him instantly.

He may have ruled with an iron fist "back in the day"— whenever "the day" was—but he showed no hint of that ruthless persona today.

"Please, have a seat." Cornelius indicated one of two chairs situated across from his desk. Before taking a seat himself, he pulled out a bottled water from a small fridge next to his desk and handed it to me. "I hope Wembley hasn't filled your head with his paranoid suspicions. Too much weed back in the eighties and nineties, I suspect."

I choked on the sip of water I'd just taken.

Alex dropped down into the seat next to mine and assumed a relaxed pose.

Cornelius continued as if I'd not been so rude as to sputter water on his beautiful desk. "A good sort, Wembley, just a little slow to see the changing times. He's convinced we're all still secretly living by the rules of fifty years past. That we're conspiring to bring back the Inquisition."

I bit my lip and kept my mouth shut. I'd been told to listen—so I was going to do my darnedest to actually listen.

My face must have given away my surprise, because Cornelius smiled with a twinkle in his eye. "A turn of phrase for harsher times. We're weren't truly so bad as the Inquisition."

Alex shifted uneasily in his seat.

"Come now, Alex. Swift justice, yes. But we tried to be as fair as the times and our circumstances allowed." Cornelius sighed. "Nowadays it's the best we can do to make sure our membership stay below the unenhanced radar, pay their taxes, and generally keep the peace amongst our own kind. It's more administrative hassle and less magical sword-swinging these days."

I blinked. Magical swords?

"But that's neither here nor there." Cornelius's eyebrows pulled together. "We have a serious matter on our hands."

And with those few words, I was in seventh grade standing before Vice Principal Swenson all over again.

Alex nudged me. "He means your rat."

"Oh. Oh! Yes." Now it was my turn to look stern, because, really, the Society had dropped the ball. "I don't think killing civilians is going to keep you guys under the unenhanced radar."

"Us," Cornelius gently corrected me. "You're a member now. You can expect your membership dues invoice to arrive shortly."

Was he kidding? I looked into his sharp blue gaze and thought most likely not. "Do I get a handbook once I'm paid up?"

"Orientation classes." Cornelius inclined his head. "But you were saying?"

I gave Alex a covert glance. Should I be jumping up and down that I'd been officially accepted? His bland expression implied "no."

I focused my full attention on Cornelius. "A string of dead women is hardly staying under the radar. What's being done? Are you investigating? Are you doing something to stop this murdering...rat?" I couldn't come up with a better descriptor. I hated rats. More than snakes. My scalp prickled. Ugh.

"The dead women, as appalling as their deaths may be, are not problematic for the Society. They all appear to have died of natural causes. It is extremely unlikely the vampire virus will be detected in their systems. While such actions would be punished should the culprit be known, in this instance we do not have a perpetrator. Neither will we have one without extensive investigation; perhaps not even then. And our resources are thin."

My blood started to boil. Liz hadn't been a friend—but she didn't deserve this. No one deserved this. And what about me? Apparently, I was chopped liver.

"Mind the eyes, dear. They've gone all red," Cornelius chided me as if I'd cut my steak with a butter knife. Slightly embarrassing, but not appalling.

"They've gone all red because I'm angry. Livid." A sharp pain in my shin brought my attention around to Alex. "Hey."

"Listen."

That was all he said, but it was enough to grab my attention and stem the tide of what would likely be regrettable words.

"Alex has brought it to my attention that you are not the only accidental transformation. There have been two others, and neither has ended well." Cornelius's voice was quite solemn. This, at least, he was taking seriously.

I shook my head. How could I have forgotten? "Dr. Dobrescu's other patient. The one that got her hooked up with the Society."

"Yes. That was a sad case. The other victim has just come to our attention. She wasn't sound enough to seek the aid of a doctor—and she couldn't stand the thirst. With no blood supply, no orientation to our world...it did not end well either." Cornelius steepled his fingers, in much the same fashion as his detractor Wembley, oddly. "Dr. Dobrescu was most helpful. She's an enlightened soul, the kind so rarely seen in our world."

I didn't remember thinking quite *that* highly of her. She'd *tried* to help me...I thought. But she'd also hustled me out the door, pulling me along behind her as fast as her clogged feet could move.

"But the risk of other accidental transformations is enough for you to find this...rat?" I couldn't find another word. The truth was a terrible thing, and rat seemed safer. And still somewhat accurate.

"It is. You and Alex seem to work nicely together."

Cornelius nodded. "Yes, you'll do. I'm prepared to offer you a small stipend."

Alex laughed. "Just so you know, this is how it starts. We'll give you this small stipend for a project. Oh, we have another. Here's yet another. Suddenly, you've got full-time employment working for the Society."

Cornelius shot Alex a disapproving look.

"Hey, it's only fair. She hasn't even gone through orientation yet and you're practicing your shady recruitment tactics on her."

I lifted a hand. "It's fine." Because, unless I was mistaken, I was being offered a paycheck to do exactly what I was already doing: finding the killer of my human-ness, pathetic and anxiety-ridden as it had been. "How much?"

"Five thousand."

I glanced at Alex. No response.

"And?" I asked.

"Expenses."

I glanced at Alex again. Again, no response.

"And?"

"With the project's completion upon apprehension of the subject or at the end of a ten-day term, wherein reasonable efforts have been made to apprehend the subject, whichever occurs first." I looked at Alex, but Cornelius cleared his throat in an attention-commanding way. "You needn't ask Alex; that's my best offer."

"Accepted."

Alex groaned.

"What? What did I miss?" My gaze flew between the two men.

"Pshaw. Nothing." Giving Alex a steely look, Cornelius said, "I'll pay her quickly. Good first impressions and such."

Alex snorted. "I won't hold my breath." He turned to me

and said, "Always include payment terms, otherwise Cornelius is likely to settle up at the end of the year."

Since I wasn't starving, that wasn't a problem. But I nodded and made a mental note.

"And reasonable is a highly subjective term," Alex said. "I suspect, if left to Cornelius's definition, reasonable effort is equivalent to apprehending the subject."

"Oh, now that's hardly fair." I scowled at Cornelius, but he just shrugged. "All right, then. How do we proceed?"

"Exactly as you started." Cornelius rose from his chair. "I wish you success. It's to no one's advantage if this misbehavior continues."

Misbehavior? But I bit my lip again.

I almost reached my hand out, but recalled that we hadn't shaken hands on meeting. "It was nice to meet you."

"Yes, good day." Cornelius sat back down and turned to the computer screen on his desk.

Alex didn't seem to mind. He stood up, stretched, then headed to the door at a casual pace. He held the door open for me but didn't immediately follow me through.

I thought I heard Cornelius say, "You're welcome," but I could have been mistaken because the words were quite faint.

Alex shut Cornelius's office door firmly behind him. "To give you a little perspective, when he says the doctor is enlightened, he means that no voodoo excisions of her memory were required. She agreed to work within the Society's rules."

My eyeballs felt like they were about ready to pop out of my skull.

"Yeah." Alex inclined his head. "The new, modern Cornelius is one part bureaucrat, one part accountant, and two parts survivalist. And those are just the parts we see."

"Fair warning—got it. And thanks."

"There's no real preparing for Cornelius, just hoping not to be blindsided."

I nodded, though I suspected that Cornelius would get the best of me on more than one occasion in the future. "Where to, partner?"

Alex stopped and turned to look at me. "Not partners. Partner implies equality, and you, baby vamp, are nowhere close."

"Where to, bossman?" Not that he was my boss—he wasn't paying me. But I could play nice.

"My office. I've got that security footage you wanted to see, and I need to have a crack at pulling up Liz's credit and debit card purchases for the last few days."

Definitely not my boss—but very helpful. And on matters of timing and the police, I might defer. My mother would never forgive me if I was arrested.

Alex's office, located close to the front of the warehouse and just around the corner from the retail store, was nothing like Cornelius's. It was much larger, but not nearly so swanky. Where Cornelius's office had an executive feel, Alex's was more lived in. Used, comfortable furniture, a larger fridge—though not quite full size—a huge desk that had a worked-in feel. A calendar hung on the wall behind the desk, and sticky notes were tacked on the edge of his monitor.

I didn't doubt that Cornelius worked in his office, but I knew Alex spent a lot of time in his.

My eyes swiveled back to the fridge. "Do you mind?" I asked, pointing to the fridge.

Alex paused a hair longer than I would have expected then said, "Help yourself."

Did wizards need blood? He'd clearly been trying to

remember what was inside. Or maybe something else disgusting, like... But my mind drew a blank. Next to blood, most stuff wasn't that gross.

I opened the door to reveal a shocking truth: Alex was a health nut. Fresh fruit and veggies, a few varieties of juice, nuts, a small container of milk, granola, yogurt, kefir, a loaf of grainy wheat bread, and a small butcher's package of deli meat.

"Keeping your bread in the fridge dries it out." I grabbed his carrot juice. "Can I have this?"

No need for him to know I hadn't tested out carrot juice yet. I'd just make a really quick run to the bathroom if it didn't agree with me.

"No problem." He'd booted up a laptop and had a file open. He turned the screen for me to see. "I've sliced out the relevant portion of the video from the original security footage and have it looped to play ten times. If you want more than that, just hit play again."

Eying the laptop, I took a quick swig of the carrot juice, counted to fifteen, and took another swig. Probably good.

Alex gave me a weird look then handed me the laptop.

I planted myself on the futon. It was much more comfortable than it looked. I situated myself in the corner and asked, "Sleep here much?"

He glanced up from his desk. He was already reading through Liz's bank statement. "Occasionally." The man had some serious work ethic. Because I was starting to learn to read between the lines, and that definitely translated to a lot.

I pressed play—and there I was. All twelve sloppy, stumbling-drunk seconds of me. "Oh. This is terrible. I look wasted. I only had two white wine spritzers, I swear!"

"Your apparent inebriated state could be explained by a drug like Rohypnol. Remember, we talked about that."

"All well and good for you to be calm. If my mother ever saw this..."

He was looking at me like I was a crazed woman—which was completely unfair. No one wanted their mother to seem them sloppy drunk.

"What? Do you not have a mother?"

"Not for a long time."

Nuts. Open mouth and insert foot—except that was where my foot seemed to be living lately. "My condolences."

"It was a long time ago." He didn't look distraught. Heck, he didn't even look up from Liz's financial records.

I'd missed the rest of the loops, so I gritted my teeth and pushed play. "Great. I will never be able to erase this. Please, please, please, never go viral." And then plastered me stumbled and steadied herself—myself—on the passenger window of a car, and a tiny light bulb went off in my brain. "Reflective surfaces. Alex, reflective surfaces!"

He looked up, shook his head, and went back to his computer.

"No, this might be it. You know, catch the bad guy with a reflection."

"That still means as little to me as it did the first time."

"Do you not watch TV?"

"Do you see a TV in here?"

What an odd thing to say. Did the man not have a home? It was one thing to sleep in his office a lot—but surely he had a home?

"Whatever. Whenever the killer has hidden his face from the camera, the tech people always try to find reflective surfaces with different angles." I was bouncing with excitement and had a near miss with Alex's laptop, so I took a breath. In a calmer tone and without bouncing, I said, "Once they have an image from a reflective surface, they can enhance the video to ID the bad guy. Voila, case closed."

"First, Sherlock, this video won't enhance. Not without sophisticated software we don't have. It'll just get grainier if we blow up the picture."

I tried not to let his naysaying dampen my spirits. Then again, he had more ammo. "And second?"

"Do you actually see any reflective surfaces?"

"I'm about to look, thank you very much. You're welcome to help, if you like." I patted the futon next to me then reset the video to play from the start of the loop.

The futon dipped when he accepted my invitation. I tipped the screen slightly to the right so he could see better.

The parking garage looked much darker on the video than it did in person. And the quality of the video wasn't the greatest. But maybe...

"There." Alex pointed at the screen. "When you wobble on your heels. Don't growl at me—you're wobbling. See, the lights from that car bounce off the window of that car." He pointed again.

"I think you're right." I hunkered down closer to the screen with my finger on pause. There—I jabbed the pause key.

We both leaned in, staring at the screen.

"What do you see?" I asked.

"What do you see?"

"Seriously?" I leaned closer. "I see...a blob."

"A not-tall blob."

I tipped my head, hoping the perspective change would help. "A not-tall, not-short blob." I groaned. "I really thought this would be more helpful."

"We have a picture. A grainy, blobby picture, but that's more than we had before."

"Can your..." I didn't know what to call them, because "spirit guides" had been a kind of joke when he'd used the term. Apparently me waggling my fingers in the air in a woo-woo fashion was sufficient.

"Spirits? Demons? Elementals?"

"Sure, if that's what you use. Can they help?"

I could swear his eyes were crinkling up in the beginnings of a smile. "With digital video enhancement? No."

How was I supposed to know that was a silly question? "Hey, I haven't even had orientation yet."

Alex snorted. "You won't learn about spirit entities in orientation."

"Ah. What exactly do I learn in orientation?"

"Where all the bathrooms are. Whoa. Wait a second. You see that shading difference?"

I squinted, leaned forward, back...maybe... "He has a beard. Ha! Our guy has a beard."

And who did I know that had a beard and had been with me on Tuesday?

"Martin. That scaly reptile."

"Martin Shade?" Alex asked. "He's not on the Society's rolls. That's all I know. I have a brief background workup on him, but I've only scanned it."

"Where? I want to see it."

Alex leaned back in the futon. "You have got to work on the eyes. Red is bad—glowing red will get you staked, dissected, or hung."

"I thought staking wasn't really a thing?"

"Better. When you're distracted, it fades." He retrieved a file from his desk and handed it to me.

"I'm allowed to be angry in the privacy of, well, of your

office." When he gave me a disapproving look, I stuck my tongue out at him. Juvenile? Yes. But oh so satisfying.

"You have to take this seriously. There can be serious consequences for behavior that exposes the Society."

"Uh-huh." I flipped through the first few pages, looking for the meaty parts. "Martin is such a reptile, but he's a reptile with a lot of debt. A lot."

"Drugs, alcohol, gambling, or student loans," Alex said. "In my experience, those are the big ones."

"Or he's just bad with money." I flipped quickly through to the end. "No student debt. Lots of maxed-out credit cards. But nowhere do I see in big red letters 'psychotic vamp.'"

"Yeah, you wouldn't, though, would you?" Alex took the file and looked through it. "Even though he's not on the rolls, he could be unregistered. He's only lived in Austin three years."

"And yet it feels like so much longer."

Alex set the file on his desk and then perched on the edge. "You really do not like this guy. What's the deal?"

"He's just nasty. He has this slick exterior that a lot of the guys at the office buy into, but he's vicious. Undermines other people's projects, takes credit for work that's not his, practically abuses his assistant—and he screwed with my career when that was still really important to me."

"None of that makes him a vampire, though he does seem to share similarities with many I've met."

"You mentioned before that vamps aren't particularly well liked, but the only one I've met seems pretty cool. Wait, Cornelius isn't—"

"No. Assassin. And Wembley's different—like you."

I wasn't sure how I felt about being different. Not until I met some of these notoriously unlikeable vamps. But that was a task for a different day, since none seemed to be lurking on the sidelines. "I think it's time I collected my personal items from the office."

Alex grinned. "Excellent plan. Would you like an escort?"

15

RATODILE

I climbed into the passenger seat without even thinking. Hard to believe I'd only driven my own car once since I bought it.

"If we hurry, I can pick up my separation packet from HR before they're gone for the day. Martin will be around for ages, but HR is deserted by five after five."

Alex grinned. "I can hurry."

"Should I be worried?" I clicked my seatbelt and then double-checked it. He looked a little too confident for my comfort.

"Wizards have exceptional dexterity—didn't I mention?"

"Pretty sure that's a no, since you hoard information like a Cold War spy."

Although that would explain why he always wanted to drive. I'd be uncomfortable riding in a car with someone who had significantly diminished reaction times—say, like drunk people.

"Ugh. I'm the drunk person." With Alex's bewilderment evident, I could hardly not explain. I sighed. "With you and me in the car together, I'm the drunk person; you're the designated driver."

"Right. Or you could just be the person who doesn't drive as well as me."

"You're so unimaginative, Alex." My fingers clutched at my purse in my lap. "And speedy."

"Don't tell a guy with enhanced vision, dexterity, strength, and speed that you're in a hurry"—he passed a van like it was standing still—"unless you want a fast ride. Besides, I've driven your car before. It's in decent shape. What's the deal with your separation packet? Does that make you officially unemployed?"

Controlled breathing seemed like a handy plan. Or praying. I compromised with a mantra. *I will arrive in one piece. I will arrive...* "Not quite. I have six weeks of accumulated vacation. So I have to decide if I'm taking that vacation or a payout for it; that will determine my termination date. My separation packet is primarily about all of the extra goodies. My retirement package, insurance—the various details involved in divorcing myself from a company that's employed me for thirteen years."

"If it makes you feel any better, you have health insurance through the Society."

"Really? Oh, wait. I don't actually need medical care, do I?"

"Not in the traditional sense. There are a few blood-borne pathogens that can have a negative impact on vamps, but screening and some basic training to recognize telltale markers in the blood eliminates most of the risk. Not an issue for you, of course."

"Cancer, high blood pressure, heart attack?"

"No, not an issue. Hanging, decapitation, starvation—"

"Stop. I don't even know in what world I have to worry

about being decapitated. Let's just save that story for later. Unless there's an immediate concern?"

"Hard to say."

"You're messing with my happy again, Alex."

He pulled into the parking lot of my soon-to-be-ex-employer. "But I got you here with fifteen minutes to spare."

"Thank you." I unclenched my fingers from my purse so I could undo my seatbelt. *Mental note: don't mention speed, being in a hurry, or deadlines when riding with Alex.*

Fifteen minutes before five meant that I caught a few stragglers in the HR department. Not to say they didn't work as hard as everyone else. I assumed they did, but they kept different hours from the mainstream of the employees. I rarely had arrived at work before nine, for example.

A nice lady named Linda gave me the packet and told me I could drop it in the mail when I was done with the forms. She gave Alex a curious look.

"I was planning to pop down and collect my personal items," I said, and tucked the packet under my arm.

"I'm her muscle." Alex waved from the doorway where he'd been lurking and gave her a friendly smile.

And that was all it took to put Linda at ease—surprise, surprise.

Once we'd parted ways with Linda and were headed to the elevator, I whispered, "That was downright normal of you."

"Please." Alex smirked. "We don't need her calling security."

"So you can pretend at normal, but don't enjoy it. How do you date so much?"

"Who says I do?" He held the elevator open for me and waited for me to step through.

I pushed the button for my floor. "Martin has a private office, so we can corner him in there and grill him."

"I just need to meet him."

"You can tell if someone is a vamp on sight?" I asked.

How had such a nugget eluded me? And, more importantly, could I learn the skill?

The elevator stopped two floors short of mine, and a woman joined us.

As we rode the elevator in stilted silence, I realized we might be minutes away from finding the rat. Or the reptile. I'd never really considered what kind of reptile Martin was.

"Don't crocodiles drown their prey?"

The woman's lips pinched in disapproval, so I flashed her the broadest, friendliest smile I could muster. It seemed the most perverse response—and I didn't work here anymore.

"I believe they do," Alex said.

Yeah, Martin was a crocodile. He snapped when you least expected it and just hung on, smothering you with his vile comments until you drowned.

The elevator dinged, announcing our arrival.

"He can't be a croc and a rat at the same time, though, can he?"

"We're about to find out." Alex pushed the "door open" button and waited for me to exit then followed behind. After the elevator doors whooshed closed, he said, "But just in case he is our rat, I brought along an old friend."

I turned to ask who, but there was no need. He had a massive sword strapped to his back.

Leaning close, I whispered, "Can everyone see that thing? It's huge."

"You'll be able to see it now, because you know it's there —but no one else should."

"And if you can hide something that big, why not something smaller...and better, like a gun?" I mouthed the last word, because the last thing I wanted was a workplace incident before we even had a chance to confront Martin. The building definitely had armed security on site, usually a few off-duty cops.

"We're not getting into guns versus magical swords right now."

"Shush with the G-word. The walls have big ears. And the security guards are armed." We'd come to the hall where all of my old division's offices were located. Including Martin's. And Liz's. My feet wouldn't move.

As soon as I stopped, the sound of my own heartbeat filled my ears. Normally, I'd be sweating about now, but I wasn't.

My heart thudded faster. My chest felt tight. I couldn't catch my breath.

"Pull it together. Your eyes are bleeding red."

My hands flew to my face.

"Not literally. Bleeding red eyes...it's just a turn of phrase."

I couldn't catch my breath, and he was worried about the stupid eye thing.

"You can't hyperventilate, and your blood pressure shouldn't drop low enough to cause lightheadedness." Alex leaned close to my face. "So get it together."

I never would have thought you could pressure or intimidate fear. It seemed counterintuitive—until I experienced it in action.

The tightness in my chest eased. And once the band around my ribcage loosened, I could breathe again. "Whew—thanks." I stood up straight, tucked my hair behind my ears, and asked, "How are my eyes?"

"Your eyes are fine. So is your hair. And your outfit."

"That is not what I meant." I turned on my heel and marched down the hallway, past my old office, past Liz's, and straight up to Martin's. The door was closed, per usual. I considered knocking, then decided that the man—rat, crocodile, whatever he was—hadn't earned the privilege. I threw the door open.

To find Martin picking his nose.

Ew. Really. Super ew.

"What are you doing here? I thought we'd seen the last of you." He grabbed a tissue from his desk and blew his nose.

Alex was at my shoulder. He whispered in my ear, "Not our guy."

A little bubble inside me popped. "Martin, you are a snotty crocodile. That's all you are."

He huffed out a derisive snort. "Your opinion means less than nothing to me. You don't even work here anymore. I heard you'd gone off the deep end." His eyes narrowed, and he gave me a look that made my skin crawl. "But they didn't say anything about you graduating from fat camp."

I tried to think happy thoughts. Distracting, not red-eyed thoughts. Because the place I'd been living since my transformation seemed to be fading and the insecurities of my past were bubbling up: what people thought of me, whether I was good enough—at my job, at life.

Alex gave my shoulder a squeeze. "Mr. Shade, we have a few questions for you."

"Seriously, why do I care?" Turning to me, Martin asked, "Who is this guy?" He rolled his chair away from the desk and crossed his hands over his stomach.

Had he always been this obtuse? Self-interested, yes. But stupid? Before, he'd seemed...not clever exactly, but savvy.

He'd been able to fool several of our coworkers into believing he was a hardworking go-getter, and that took some skill, given he was neither hardworking nor good at his job.

But now I wondered. Hindsight was so much clearer. It made me wonder how distorted the lens I viewed him through had been. Maybe others had seen him as he was... and I simply hadn't noticed.

Which explained why I'd been his frequent target. Why he'd sabotaged my client relationships. The reptile had started a rumor that I was a sex addict. Our clientele tended to be somewhat conservative—so that had been problematic, not to mention embarrassing.

I could feel myself getting angry...and then I wasn't. Why did I care about this man? I certainly no longer cared about the career he'd tried to damage. Oh, and he'd failed at that anyway. He was an insignificant toad. I choked back a snort. So much better than a crocodile.

Once I'd gotten a handle on my newfound toad-inspired amusement, I said, "Answer a few questions, and we'll leave. Simple as that." Giving him the evil eye, I added, "For Liz, if nothing else."

But his face had a stubborn cast. I suspected he was calculating the worth of his knowledge and exactly what he could squeeze out of this situation.

"Mr. Shade, Martin, if you don't answer our questions, I'm sure security will be more than pleased to search your desk for certain missing items." Alex's gaze darted briefly to the ceiling. "A Mrs. Margery Holt's credit card, a Mont Blanc pen, and a rather pricey ballerina figurine."

Martin had gone pale under his beard. "What... How... Uh, I have no idea what you mean. I don't really have time for this, so if you want me to answer your questions, you better hurry it up." By the time he'd muddled through his response, he'd regained his composure.

But I didn't doubt Alex had very accurate insider knowledge. There were spirits involved in this magic trick, I'd wager.

"Tuesday," Alex said. "Tell me what you did."

"Went to work, had lunch with a buddy, drinks after work, watched a movie, went to bed." He got a little twitchy when he mentioned the movie.

My guess: it was porn.

But Alex homed in on it. "What movie?"

"I don't know." Sweat gathered at his temple.

Alex didn't do anything—he just stood there. Maybe he exuded a menacing air, or maybe Martin's own guilt was enough to loosen his tongue, but he finally said, "I gambled. Most of the night. No movie, just online gambling."

I didn't understand what the big secret was. "Why lie—"

"He's an addict, that's why." Alex gave Martin a hard look. "Right?"

Martin ran a hand through his hair. "I'm on a trial separation with my wife. One of the conditions to us getting back together is that I don't gamble."

Aw. Martin actually cared about someone besides himself.

"I cannot afford a divorce. She can't find out I've been gambling." Martin ran his hand through his hair again, and it stuck up at odd angles.

And then again, maybe not. How had I ever seen this miserable toad as a threat?

I sighed. "What about the stealing? You think she'd be okay with that?"

Martin's eyes had a wild look. "Why are you guys asking

me these questions? And what does this have to do with Liz?"

"She's—" I shut up when Alex nudged my leg. That was better than kicking my shin, and it was always a good idea to reward good behavior. So I bit my tongue.

"Tell us about getting drinks after work." As he spoke, Alex moved around to the other side of Martin's desk, crowding him.

Martin rolled his chair further away "What are you..."

"Drinks?" Alex pulled out the items he'd listed earlier. I even recognized the little ballerina. It belonged to Shelley; she'd kept it on her desk.

Martin swallowed. "We went for drinks. Mallory was always good for one or two rounds."

"And?" Alex moved toward the door, giving Martin a little more room.

But it didn't make him any more comfortable. His eyes kept darting from me to his stolen stash, now in Alex's hands. "And we drank. That's what people do when they go for drinks."

"Who was there?" Alex asked.

Now he was starting to look worried, but in a different way. His attention moved from the stolen stash to me. "Me, Mallory, Shelley, Penelope, and Liz. Same as always."

"Did anything unusual happen?"

"You are seriously freaking me out. What's going on?"

Alex glanced at me, and I took my cue. "I was attacked on Tuesday. And Liz—" My throat started to close up. I swallowed and tried to stave off the tears. I could not have an acid-tear incident in Martin's office.

"Liz is dead," Alex said, giving me a funny look.

"Dead? No, she was here...Friday, she was here at work."

The little snot didn't even blink at me being attacked—but the gorgeous Liz...

Oh, wow. I was a truly terrible person. She had died. I'd been about a half-second away from crying acid tears over her loss. I was still here, and I'd gotten a second chance. An opportunity to shed some baggage. I thought the baggage was gone—but clearly this little scene in Martin's office had disproved that assumption. Baggage still remaining—but perhaps packed up tidily and ready to be disposed of? I just need to give it a tiny little push...

"She's dead now," I said. "And my neighbor, a lovely old lady with lots of friends, she's dead, too. And that's why you're going to act like a human being for a change and answer our questions. You're going to tell us everything about Tuesday. About the last time you saw Liz. About anything unusual that's happened in the last few days. Okay?" I ended my tirade with a very satisfying finger jab in his direction.

"Sure. Okay."

And he did. For thirty minutes, he went over everything he could think of. Unfortunately, it wasn't worth squat.

Martin tended to pay attention to things that affected Martin. That limited his observational data pool. On top of that, not much interesting appeared to have happened. Life had been as usual. On Tuesday, the group had stayed for one more round and then gone home. No drama ensued, no interesting tidbits of gossip were shared, no particularly outstanding events transpired.

"What about the bartender?" Alex asked.

"What about him?" Martin looked confused.

"It's possible Mallory was drugged. Did you notice anything about the bartender or the people standing next to Mallory?"

"Like what?"

"Did any of them have a beard?" I asked. You'd think I'd know, but Rohypnol...

"A lot of guys had beards—the hip kind. It was that kind of crowd." Alex gave Martin another hard look. "Okay—maybe a guy on your left who ordered for himself and his buddy. Definitely one of the bartenders, but no clue which one served us."

"Anything else?" Alex asked.

"No. Can I have my, ah, that stuff back?" Martin's beady little eyes held that vicious light I'd seen so many times.

But now, knowing what I did, I'd wager it was panic. He'd been running around, stealing from coworkers, hiding a gambling problem from everyone at work and his wife—the guy had to be living in a constant state of fear.

I was a nincompoop. An unobservant ninny.

"Bye, Martin," I said. "With any luck at all, we'll never see each other again. Oh, and we will be turning these items into the security desk downstairs on our way out. Good luck with that."

He grabbed his computer bag and left—hair sticking up in odd angles and sweat stains visible on his shirt. How had I ever seen *that guy* as a crocodile?

"Bye-bye." I waved at him as he left. Once he was far enough along the hall that he couldn't hear, I said, "I'll just return these to the appropriate offices."

"He doesn't deserve it."

"I know."

By the time we were finished with Martin, just about everyone on the floor had left. Except Shelley. I'd bet cash she was still in the office, because she usually kept late hours.

The figurine in my fingers felt cool and fragile. I glanced at it, hesitating to turn the corner toward Shelley's office.

Why was it more difficult to face the one coworker who was actually a decent person?

I cringed when I realized it might have something to do with my own behavior.

Loosening my grip on the delicate ceramic piece between my fingers, I lifted it and said, "Shelley."

Alex gave me a sympathetic look, but he didn't say anything. Sometimes, he was a decent guy.

16

PUSHING THE BAGGAGE...INTO A BLACK HOLE

I knocked on Shelley's open door and poked my head in.

"Hi." She looked more than a little surprised to see me.

"I think this is yours?" I placed the tiny dancing woman on her desk.

She frowned, confused. "Where...?"

Alex stepped into the office to hand me the two other stolen items, and then said, "I'll just head over to your office and box up your personal things."

I smiled my thanks and turned back to Shelley...who was leaning in her chair to watch Alex walk away.

"Yeah, he's kinda cute, isn't he?"

Shelley raised her eyebrows. "More like smoking hot." Her face flushed. "I'm sorry—is he your boyfriend?"

"No. No, definitely not. He's...ah, he's a friend." And he was. One of the few I had at the moment. Dragon-stingy with his little golden eggs of information, but he was my friend.

"Hmm."

I sat down in the only other chair in the office. "And no, I will not give him your number. My worlds have collided enough for one day."

Shelley laughed. "Sorry. Pickings are a little slim at the office. With the exception of Martin, everyone on this floor is married. And Martin..." She shuddered.

And then I realized—I'd had no clue he was married, and he didn't wear a ring. "You know he's married?"

"No." Shock permeated her voice. "Wow. The levels that guy will sink."

"Yeah, speaking of that—can you return these? Martin also has some debt issues, which has resulted in sticky fingers." I reached across the desk and handed her the credit card and the Mont Blanc pen.

Her gaze traveled to the figurine, and her eyes briefly closed. "It was a gift from my nana. I really should bring it home. But who would have thought..." She accepted the items then lifted the pen and said, "Dave Tanaka's. He was groaning about it going missing a few days ago. I'll return them tomorrow."

"And Martin?"

"I'm not sure." Worry lines appeared on her forehead and her lips thinned. "I have to work with him."

Maybe I hadn't been the guy's only target. Ugh. Disgusting. Shelley was *nice*. "If you go to HR and lodge a complaint, I have a log of the few things he's done that I can actually prove."

Shelley wrinkled her nose. "Not the sex addict thing, though."

I laughed. Because in retrospect, it was funny. I mean, not addiction, and not alienating my clients...but that he'd tag me as the addict, when all along he had the gambling problem. And to make me a sex addict... I snorted and then let out a massive belly laugh.

Shelley's face squished up for a second and then she let loose, too.

She wiped her eyes and grinned at me. "You've changed. Quitting was good for you."

That sobered me. "Yes, it was definitely the right choice." Unfortunately, I'd needed a nasty little virus to help me do it.

"I hate to comment—but have you lost a lot of weight since I saw you, um, a week or so ago?"

I sighed. "Long story, but how about we stick with: it was the flu."

"Sure thing." She didn't seem too bothered by the explanation—or was too polite to say more.

I looked at her, and I tried to see her—not the person I'd thought her to be when I was so consumed by work, so worried about paying bills that I had more than enough money to pay. I'd thought she was okay before, but she was a really nice woman. "I'm sorry, Shelley. For being..." I closed my eyes. Being what? Being myself? When I opened them, she gave me a grim look.

"No. I am. We all knew how terrible Martin was, how much this job means—meant—to you." She shrugged. "It was hard to see past the rough edges, but we should have tried. *I* should have tried."

And that's when I kicked my baggage over the edge where it had been teetering since my transformation. "Thank you. I'm working on embracing my happy—and it's having a positive effect, I think. I highly recommend it."

She grinned again. "Embrace my happy. I'll try."

She hadn't been on the interrogation list, but thinking

about it now, I wasn't sure why. Shelley was a much more reliable source than Martin.

"Do you mind if I ask you a few questions? About the Tuesday night we went out for drinks?"

She looked a little taken aback. "Sure, no problem." Then a strange look came over her face. "That was the last time we saw you, before you got the flu."

"That's right." My gaze darted away from her. I really had to work on my poker face. "Did anything weird happen after I left? Or did you notice anything odd before I left?"

"Nothing unusual. Some guy hit on Liz and got a little rowdy when she wasn't interested. That was right after you left. But his friend calmed him down, and they left."

"Any chance either of them had a beard?"

"The friend did. Why? What's going on? Liz wasn't at work today...has something happened?"

I took a breath but no words emerged. They two women had clearly been close. I'd had no idea. And I certainly hadn't planned to give Shelly news of her good friend's death. A death I wasn't supposed to even know about. Nuts.

Shelly gave me a sympathetic look. "Are you okay? Did something happen? Is that why you haven't been at work?" She bit her lip. "I'm sorry. If you don't want to talk about it—"

"No, no it's fine." She'd given the perfect excuse, lord love her. "Someone attacked me, and I'm trying to find out who it was."

Shelley leaned forward, her forearms pressed against the edge of her desk. "That's terrible. What are the police doing?"

"I'm trying really hard to learn more, but I haven't involved the police. I just can't."

Shelley looked like she might cry. For me.

My eyes started to burn. I had to stop that train wreck. "I'm fine. Really. I'm just so angry. I mean, really angry. Angry enough to spit."

"I'm so sorry. Anything I can do...you just have to say."

"Well, about Liz, I think maybe it's someone that has something to do with her." And I could have smacked myself. How would I explain that?

"Ah, okay..." Shelley gave me a quizzical look. But she didn't ask. Because she was a nice person, and I'd just admitted to being attacked.

Ugh. I felt terrible now. In for a penny, and all that. "I know Liz can have, um, maybe not the best...uh—"

"Exceptionally bad taste in men. Yes." Shelley sighed and then said, "There is a lot more to her than her bad taste in men. But if there's some connection to that," she paused briefly to see if I'd elaborate. When I didn't , she said, "She was seeing a married man up until about two weeks ago. He said he was leaving his wife, then he suddenly remembers he has kids and realizes he doesn't hate his wife—you know the story."

I didn't; not really. But I just asked, "Do you know his name?"

"Allen. No idea on the last name."

"Any chance he has a beard?"

"I never actually met him. Never saw any pictures. I don't really see how her ex could have anything to do with what happened to you. And there wasn't anyone new since Allen. I would have known. She glowed when she met someone new." She rolled her eyes and smiled. "She may make bad choices, but I guarantee she didn't make any trouble for him. She's not like that. She wouldn't call the house, or threaten to tell his wife. Nothing that would create any tension after the breakup."

Shelley had known a much more complex person in Liz than I had. People were flawed, but they were more than their flaws. Maybe I hadn't always bothered to see that.

I was about to wrap up the conversation, when she said, "I do remember that he works at a car dealership. She met him when she bought her car. Does that help?"

"Absolutely. Thank you." I turned to leave, but she stopped me.

She looked uncertain again. "Maybe you should consider getting in touch with the police? I think they might be able to help you." Her eyes turned bright and shiny with tears again. "I'm so sorry that happened to you."

I hadn't been the recipient of much sympathy over my situation—primarily because I could only talk to people inside the Society—but even so, the sympathy had been pretty slim. And she sounded genuinely upset on my behalf. "He didn't..." I stopped and cleared my throat. "I wasn't raped."

My face warmed with a shame I couldn't understand when I said the word out loud.

Shelley got up, walked around her desk and hugged me. Even though I knew it was coming, the feel of her arms around me was still surprising.

"I'm sorry someone hurt you, whatever happened." She gave me a last squeeze and let go.

Her reassurance made me angry all over again at my progenitor. I was going to kick him in his dangly bits, when I caught him.

Shelley caught my gaze, and her lips twitched. "I know that look. My money is on you."

"Thank you—for everything." I didn't know what else to say.

And as I walked out of her office, I realized I'd

misjudged not one, but two people. I was glad that I might be able to help find Liz's killer—to do something for the dead woman I'd so underestimated.

But putting things right would involve some vigilante justice, old-school style, and I could only hope that Shelley wouldn't mention me to the police.

17

MY FIRST SLEEPOVER...BASICALLY

I found Alex in my office, but he wasn't packing. Someone—likely my former assistant—had packed all of my personal items in a box and labeled it with my name.

Alex was sitting at my desk, tapping away on his phone. Not really sure how he could sit in that chair with a sword on his back. Magic? I'd have to ask. But then the box on the desk caught my eye for the second time.

I looked at the box and couldn't believe that was it. It made me sad that, after thirteen years, all of my things fit into one box.

"You're not going to cry, are you? Because I wasn't kidding when I said vamps don't cry."

"Big myth. We do, but the tears burn like fire."

Alex gave me a curious look then said, "Did you make nice with your ex-coworker?"

"Better than that. I have a name for you: Allen. Liz's most recent lover, former by two weeks. As amicable a split as those things can be, it sounds like—but he was and still is married."

"Any other information about Allen—a last name or where we might find him?"

I smiled. "As a matter of fact, I do believe we can track him down. I know where he works." Only because Liz had been lazy about removing the license plate frame on her new Mini, but I'd take what I could get.

"Bearded?"

"No idea, but how about we find out?" I checked the time on my phone. They'd be open for another few hours, but I had to get some food first.

Alex grabbed the box from my desk—my old desk—and said, "Let's get out of here and get you some food. We can hit Allen tomorrow. If it truly was an amicable split, then he's not a high-priority candidate."

"And if it wasn't?" I hadn't even known Liz and Shelley were friendly enough to share personal information, so I could hardly gauge whether Liz would have revealed her deepest, darkest secrets to Shelley.

"He can still wait. We need to hit the bar next door, and a little food wouldn't hurt." He exited the office. "Besides, if you know where he works, I can probably pull a history on him. See if he's on the membership rolls, has any crossover with the other victims, that type of thing. But mostly you need to tank up on some juice."

Maybe he didn't want to see me cranky. Since I could only agree that me hungry was a bad thing, I could hardly complain.

"Food is good." My stomach twisted around in a hungry knot. I'd been ignoring it pretty successfully up until now. "Actually, food is a brilliant idea."

We made our way down the elevator and out the door without encountering any curious coworkers or questioning security guards. Almost a shame, as I would have likely given in to impulse and reported Martin. But I'd let Shelley make that ultimate decision. I hadn't exaggerated about my log, though, or my willingness to step up and provide evidence of his inappropriate behavior.

After stowing my box in the Jeep, we made our way to the bar on foot. It wasn't far from the office, hence its popularity with my former coworkers.

I flagged a bartender down and asked what type of ice cream drink she recommended.

"Hold that thought." Alex smiled at the bartender and said, "We need just a moment."

"Do you want bleeding eyes?" I fluttered my lashes at him. "You like how I picked up the lingo?"

"Good job." He looked as if he was restraining himself from rolling his eyes. "Have you actually had milk?"

Ah. That was an excellent question. Great-Auntie Lula had gone all vegan in her final years. Something about how consuming the flesh and excretions of animals made her stomach churn. And on the sly, she told me it gave her horrible gas. Great-Auntie Lula liked to overshare as she got older.

I wrinkled my nose at him. "Great-Auntie Lula's drinks are vegan."

"Exactly. No milk. How about your coffee? When you went on that binge the other night..."

"I drink it black, sometimes with sugar. Oh, I did have just a tiny little taste of milk in my tea earlier today. Bradley and I were celebrating Mrs. Arbuthnot, so we thought we'd drink our tea like her."

"How much?"

"Well, I cheated a bit. I don't actually like milk in tea, but it seemed the right thing—"

"How much?"

I grumbled and finally said, "A lot less than an ice cream drink." I flagged the waitress down. "A double virgin bloody Mary."

She looked confused for a second, then asked, "So is that two virgin Marys?"

I pointed a finger at her. "You got it."

The waitress, a cute early-twenty-something with blonde hair and great big brown eyes, turned to Alex and leaned over the counter. Definitely displaying cleavage. "What can I get *you*?"

"Club soda," he replied without any inflection. She'd have to be pretty brave to try again after that reception.

She scooted away to retrieve our drinks.

"What's the look for?"

"You, not flirting with Ms. Cleavage there."

He frowned at her. "No reason to. Besides, we're here on business."

The bouncy blonde came back with three drinks, but only one of the coasters had her number on it. What was it about Alex that women found so fascinating? He wasn't that good-looking. Passable...more than passable. In the right light, quite attractive. All right, maybe hot, but not so drop-dead gorgeous as to attract the female attention that he did.

Alex paid her and included a hefty tip. "My girlfriend lost her keys on Tuesday a week ago. Any chance you've found a set?"

"No, sorry." She didn't look the least deflated when she heard about his supposed girlfriend. Either I wasn't selling it, or she had a lot of confidence.

"Do you know who was working then? Maybe we can ask if they saw anything."

The bouncy blonde tipped her head as she considered

the question. "Stacy, Joe, and Bart. I'll run and ask Joe real quick. He's in the back checking stock."

Alex lifted a hand, delaying her departure. "I'm sorry—which one is Joe? Is he the one with the beard?"

"Oh, no. That's Bart."

"Right, of course." Alex flashed her a charming smile. "Thanks."

Once she was gone, I couldn't help pointing out the problem. "One bartender with a beard, but that still leaves how many bearded patrons? Some of whom actually spoke with me or Liz, apparently."

The task was looking more and more impossible. I sucked on my virgin Mary. I'd forgotten to tell her to tone down the spice a little, but I liked the tang. And it didn't make my eyes water—thank goodness—or my nose run like spicy foods normally did.

"Bart isn't that common of a name. I can at least check the Society's rolls for a Bart or a Bartholomew."

"And now?"

"Now, I run you by your house to pack a bag and then drop you off with Wembley for the night. You need to stuff your face, because I can tell you've lost weight today. And I have a late dinner date I don't want to miss."

Aha—I knew it. "We can't just give up."

"We're not giving up. We're taking a break. And keeping you out of the rampaging killer's sights. I'll check on any possible Barts on the Society's rolls, and we'll reconvene in the morning when we're both rested."

I slurped up the last of the first bloody Mary and started to chug the second. It was *really* good. "K."

The bartender came back to tell us Joe didn't remember seeing any keys, and said that Bart and Stacy weren't sched-uled that evening, but she'd ask them tomorrow.

"No worries. I'm sure they'll turn up. Thanks for asking, though." Alex had barely touched his club soda, and he looked like he was leaving.

Yep. Definitely leaving.

"Wait just a second." I gave up on the straw and gulped down the last of the second drink. I wasn't leaving any of that tangy goodness behind.

Alex shook his head, then pulled out his phone and made a call. As I practically licked the glass clean and considered flagging the waitress down for another, Alex spoke in low tones on the phone.

I must have had a hungry-desperate look, because the waitress came back. "Another?"

Alex shook his head and then said to me, "Wembley's expecting you."

I swallowed a groan as the waitress disappeared. "Do I really need a babysitter?" Then I remembered: Mrs. A. The memory of her death came and went. I'd forget— No, not forget—it wouldn't be at the front of my brain. Then it would be there—the reality that she was gone. "Never mind. Thanks." I hurried to catch up as Alex headed to the exit.

"Wembley's glad for the company." He opened the front door for me. "His business partner, who was also his room-mate, just left Austin for Chicago. He won't say, but he hates living alone."

"I don't suppose he lives in the suburbs?" I got into the passenger seat of my car and buckled up.

Wembley did in fact live in the suburbs, as I discovered when I plugged the address Alex gave me into the map on my phone. He lived in a small neighborhood not far from the Society's headquarters, if my GPS wasn't lying.

After a rather silly discussion that lasted much of the drive to my condo, wherein I argued my ability to drive from point A (my townhome) to point B (Wembley's home) and pointed out that in doing so, Alex could reclaim his own car and therefore be more likely to make his date on time, finally, Alex agreed to let me venture off alone. But it had taken most of the drive for me to talk him around to the practicality of that option.

He'd still insisted on accompanying me upstairs, and stood in my condo and waited for me to pack toiletries—that I suspected I did not need—and my meager supply of correctly sized clothes. He then escorted me to my car and even closed the driver's door for me. I felt like a sixteen-year-old off on her first overnight trip. All that was missing was seeing him wave in my rearview mirror as I drove away.

But when I looked back, he was in his car, talking on his phone. Likely with his hot date.

Good thing I wasn't sixteen and in love, or my feelings might have been hurt.

It took me about twenty minutes to get to Wembley's neighborhood. After that, it was all over. I became that Sunday driver that everyone hates. The one who drives five miles an hour and stops to look at every passing butterfly. And my butterflies were "For Sale" signs.

House, for sale, in Austin. The kind of house that had a sign out front actually advertising the house for sale. Not the kind where the realtor puts the sign out saying the listing will be coming soon...and then the house is snapped up before you can blink.

I thought I might be in heaven.

A heaven with intermittently overgrown lawns, lots of street-parked cars, and a great number of visible trash cans. But it spoke to me. I wasn't sure if it was saying "buy a house" or if it was saying "rent"—but it was speaking.

As I pulled into Wembley's drive, I got a text from Alex: *Where are you?*

I replied: *Wembley's. Why? Where are you?*

I could imagine the exasperated look on his face as I read his response: *Did you walk?*

Have fun with your girlfriend. Bye-bye. I pressed send with a smirk.

I grabbed my tiny overnight bag and marched up to the door. It was an unpleasant brown orange, and peeling. Wembley needed to have a look at it.

Wembley opened the door before I could knock. "Thank goodness. I thought Alex was going to cancel his plans and drive out here if you were any longer." He opened the door wide and stepped to the side. "Welcome to Casa Wembley."

A ladder rested against the wall, and I had to sidestep to squeeze by it. Half the popcorn had been removed from the hallway ceiling, and tarps were spread on the ground to catch most of the mess.

"Alex didn't tell me you were redecorating. I'm so sorry to put you out."

"No, not at all. I'm always redecorating. I flip houses for grins—and free housing, but mostly for grins." He lifted the drink in his hand. "Margarita?"

This neighborhood, this house, seemed like the perfect answer to my current housing dilemma.

"I would absolutely love a margarita. But I'd also like to know a little more about this house."

Wembley pulled a pitcher from the fridge. "No need to hide your eyes every time I pop the fridge open. I have some fully human contractors, so no blood in the kitchen. The good stuff is in the garage." He pulled out a key on a chain from under his shirt. "Inconvenient—but such is the life of a house flipper."

"Ahhh..." Blood. Refrigerating in the garage. Under lock and key. "Uhhh..."

"Close your mouth. You may have your hang-ups with the sweet human juice that gives me life—but you have to get over that if you want to have any vamp friends." His expressive eyebrows squinched together, as if they had a mind of their own and were considering the very nature of life. "Not that most vamps are worth the trouble, but the concept is sound."

"Sorry." I gave him my shamefaced look, but only got a quirked eyebrow in response.

"On the bright side, I do have a grocery delivery coming by this evening, so you won't starve. I thought we'd experiment a little with your diet—maybe expand it."

I took the plastic cup he handed me. "So I'm your science experiment, huh?"

"Absolutely. But also, your little sunken cheeks make me want to fatten you up."

"That sounds a little too Hansel and Gretel to be comforting."

"Whoa, nelly. You know vamps can't feed off each other, right? Not quite poisonous, but upsets the digestion." He patted his paunchy stomach.

"I did not know that, but it's an interesting factoid."

He invited me to sit in one of the folding lawn chairs he had set up around a card table in the kitchen.

I plopped down into what was probably the most comfortable lawn chair I had ever occupied.

"Nice, right? My friend makes them; I can hook you up. But about the house—what do you want to know?"

"When's it up for sale, how much, all the dirt...everything."

"Alex told me you were looking to move. Are you asking

for yourself?" I nodded, and he said, "You don't want this one. I have another one that I just finished up. It's going on the market as soon as I get done packing up. I've been living there until the renovations on this one were far enough along for me to move in—and since they just finished up the master bath, here I am."

"So you move from house to house to house..."

Wembley shrugged. "Not always. I move when it suits me. I'm experiencing a footloose and fancy-free mood currently."

I finished off my margarita and wondered when exactly those groceries would be arriving. My stomach seemed to have a personality of its own now. A demanding, tetchy personality. "Wait a second, how long has this particular mood lasted?"

He scratched his beard. "2008, or was it 2010? More than five years, less than ten. As long as I break even, I'm happy—but I usually make a little money."

Clearly, Wembley had some other means of support. I hated to ask, but at some point, someone was going to have to explain how long we lived, stayed hidden, paid taxes.

"The new bathroom is gorgeous. I'll give you a tour in a bit."

The doorbell rang, and Wembley rubbed his hands together. "Groceries!"

But he didn't head straight for the front door. He detoured to the kitchen, pulled a revolver out of one of the drawers, and said, "Wait here."

"No way." I wasn't missing how this was going down. What the heck was he thinking?

"All right, at least open the door for me if I ask."

"Will do."

"Just a minute!" Wembley hugged the hall wall and motioned for me to do the same. "Who is it?"

"Hey, Mr. Wembley. It's Chris from the grocery store. I have your delivery."

Wembley inhaled deeply, seemed satisfied with the result, and proceeded to check the peephole. He tucked the revolver in his waistband, pulled his shirt over the resulting bulge, and opened the door. "Good to see you again, Chris." He pulled some crumpled bills out of his front pocket and handed them to the kid after I'd taken the box he was carrying.

"I've got one more in the car, sir."

"I'll just walk on out with you." Wembley motioned for me to stay inside.

He came back a few moments later carrying the second box of groceries. "Do you have no sense of self-preservation?"

"Do you really keep a gun in your kitchen drawer?" I closed the front door behind him and picked up the first box from where I'd deposited it in the hallway.

"It's the only weapon I have that I can still use competently. Swords take regular practice, useful as they are. Guns as well, but less so. I'm low-key these days. I stay out of the major conflict zones. But Alex said carry a weapon."

"Do we live in the same city? What major conflict zones?"

"It's not about geography—not usually. It's about allegiances." Wembley stashed the revolver back in the kitchen drawer. "Remind me to put that thing back in the safe tomorrow. I'd hate for one of the workers to stumble on it. It would completely ruin the chill, hippie vibe I have going."

"Right, because that's the biggest concern with an unsecured weapon in your house."

"Don't judge; it's not a good look on you." He scratched his beard. "Any chance you can handle a sword? I might have just the thing—"

"No."

"You don't know until you try. It might be fun." He waggled his eyebrows.

"I'm starving. Food experimentation first, and if I'm not too exhausted from puking my guts up—I'll have a look."

"Ha!" Wembley clapped his hands. "I knew it. I can tell. There's a little precog in my family." He tapped the side of his nose.

"Sure thing, Wembley. So what did you get?" I started to root around in the box I'd placed on the new granite counter. "Eggs—are you thinking eggnog?"

"Sure. Let's do eggnog." He looked taken with the idea.

"Did you have any kind of plan?"

"Nope. Just picked out a bunch of stuff and figured we'd give it a go. But I do have a primo food processor that will just about liquefy stone. So I think we're set up for success here."

And it turned out that we were set up for success. Mostly. Raw beef, cooked beef, any kind of beef, even if pureed until it looked like vile soup gone bad—no luck.

I really used to love beef. We gave it enough tries that I inadvertently subjected myself to aversion therapy, so beef was off the menu for the foreseeable future. Eggnog tasted fabulous going down, less so coming up. But we had great luck with fruits and veggies. And spinach and mangos were especially appealing. Much more so than in my previous, fully human life. The vegan cheese didn't come back up, but it was rough going down. The smell alone almost convinced me not to eat it. Figured that would be one of the winners.

I would hardly call the feeling I experienced satiation,

but after we put a solid dent in the fruit and vegetable supply Wembley had ordered, I was almost not hungry.

"I think there has to be a way to add in some fats and protein. Those should help you feel more satisfied."

"And I need more calories. I can't eat nonstop all day to fulfill my calorie requirements. I need something densely packed with nutrients and calories. I think that's why the vegan nutrition supplement shakes were helping a little."

Wembley scribbled on a pad of paper. "A list of dos and don'ts and never-ever-agains."

I took it and pocketed it. "Perfect. Thank you. I'm in a positively buoyant state of mind. There's some kind of food in my future, which is very good news."

"Buoyant sounds like a good state of mind to meet a sword or two. Come on."

Wembley headed for the garage, and I balked.

"No chance you've stashed your swords with the blood..."

"No. It's fine. Come on." He opened the garage door and said over his shoulder, "I've got a good feeling about this."

I followed him into the dark garage feeling a little like the kid who said yes to the candy.

Then the lights came on, and all I could do was stare. He'd revamped the roomy two-car garage to be one part place to park your car and one part incredibly cool workshop.

"Aren't you worried about all of this being in the garage?"

"Nah. I've got a separate window unit to run when it's steamy—you know, six months out of the year—and I think that'll keep it reasonably comfortable."

"I meant theft, but that's also good to know."

"No, it's pretty secure. New anti-theft garage doors.

Trying to be security conscious and all that. That's why I've got the blood and the swords out here."

"You have more than one sword." I shook my head. "And what's with the swords? I'd think guns would be much more useful."

"Bite your tongue." Wembley unlocked a chest and pulled out a sword and scabbard. "This one is a beauty."

I nodded in appreciation, though all I could see was the embossed leather scabbard. Then he pulled out a second, much more worn—battered, even—scabbard.

I reached for it.

"Careful now," he said, removing it from my reach. "Introductions should always be respectful, and that means no grabbing."

If his hands hadn't been full of sword, I suspected he would have smacked my hand.

"Sorry."

And it was the second time he'd referenced the sword as if it were a person. Who met a sword or was introduced? Vamp culture was so weird. I bit my tongue and waited.

"Tangwystl. That's the name of this particular sword. We'll just give her a second to see if she has any interest in you."

I pinched my lips together.

"What? Spit it out."

"Her?"

"That's right. She's alive. Well, as alive as magic can make her." He pulled the sword from its protective casing. And I could swear I heard soft singing, foreign words whispered then gone.

Wembley smiled. "I think she might like you." He offered her the sword, hilt first. "Go ahead."

Without grabbing, I reached for the handle and

wrapped my fingers carefully around it. It felt lovely. As if it was weightless, yet had a solid heft. As if I could hold it in my hand forever, but hack a giant in half. It was a giddy feeling.

Light shone off the etchings in the metal—no, the etchings themselves shone.

"Is this sword glowing?"

"I told you she likes you. I think you're about to be adopted."

I tore my eyes away from the greenish-blue fire that seemed to swirl and dance, tracing each symbol as if it was re-etching the markings as I watched. "Adopted?"

"Would you like this sword? Quickly—don't think; just answer."

"Yes." My eyes turned back to the fiery blue-green display.

"Thank the gods. I've been looking for a home for her for ages. Poor thing has been in the trunk for a few decades, at least."

18

MY FIRST MAGIC SWORD EVER

"I'm sorry—did you just say you locked her up? In a chest? She's *alive,* and you stowed her like some old high school trophy? Shame on you."

As I spoke, Wembley shifted uncomfortably. "In fairness, I don't think her sense of time is like ours...?" He shrugged halfheartedly.

...lovely...pretty...kind...

"Um, can she speak English?"

Wembley looked at me with wide, innocent eyes. "Only if you can."

I swallowed a grumble. "And her name, Tangwystl, that's English, Welsh, Scottish?"

"Welsh."

Finally, a simple, straightforward answer.

"So she's Welsh?"

"How would I know? She's not *my* sword."

I could feel a growl growing in my chest. I had a passing thought as to whether my eyes might possibly be red.

...pretty...blue...pretty...

"Aw. Thanks." I smiled at Wembley. "She says I have pretty blue eyes."

"A sword that flatters." Wembley didn't seem to know what to say about that. Eventually he sucked air through his teeth, and said, "I can tell you that I suspect she predates her Welsh name. She's a takouba."

I scrunched up my nose. "I don't know what that is." I traced the scrollwork with the tip of my finger and whispered to Tangwystl, "Sorry."

She might have purred.

"Right. The takouba is not a Welsh sword. Might look European, but she isn't. Google it. Maybe Taureg—but I couldn't say. Each time she's come to me, she's been Tangwystl."

Best name

"You can't hear her, can you?" When he shook his head, I said, "I think that's her favorite name. Wait—each time? What does that mean?"

Wembley sighed. "She keeps coming back. As finicky as she is with her partners, you'd think they'd last longer. Although, come to think of it, you might be the first vamp." Wembley peered at me. "You're definitely the first vamp. She likes a certain type—and vamps don't usually fit the bill."

I fingered the scrollwork again. "And what type is that?"

He considered the question. "Someone with a certain zest for life."

I pursed my lips. "Zest...is that a nice way to say rambunctious enthusiasm?"

"It's a compliment. Take it and run." Wembley packed away the first blade he'd removed, a much larger one than Tangwystl.

"So, let's assume that her partners aren't dropping like

flies—just living natural human-length lives. Why and how does she get back to you?"

"Magic." I gave him a peeved look, and he said, "Fine. One time through the post. Actually messenger, because there wasn't a postal system. And another time she showed up as loot in a raid. Another time she was a gift from a grateful...ah, lady friend. Another time—"

"Whoa. That's enough; I get the picture." I couldn't help picturing Wembley with his lady friend. Thankfully my imagination steered away from nudity—but even so, I quickly shifted focus to the second question. "Any thoughts on why? Why she keeps coming back to you when you're not the partner she wants? Uh—you're not, are you?"

"Oh, definitely not. Do I seem full of zest? But you'll have to ask her why me. We don't chat."

"Oh, yeah." I'd forgotten that he couldn't hear her. "But if she doesn't talk to you, how do you know what she wants and who's a good fit?"

"A feeling. She can communicate, but not with words. And the sparkly lights were hard to miss this time around." When he saw the look on my face, he grinned. "That's not typical. But really, enough with the sword already. Let's have a look at your room."

"Wait. How am I supposed to use a sword? And how do I carry a sword around in Austin?"

"Enough with the questions. I think I'm getting a migraine—and I don't get headaches. Look, she's yours now. So the how is between the two of you." Wembley locked the trunk. "Ah—I *can* tell you that she can cloak herself. The vixen was cloaked for about three years, and I thought I'd lost her. Probably trying to teach me a lesson, put a bug in my ear to hurry up and find her a new partner. Not like it's easy to find candidates that fit the— See, there you go."

The sword in my hand had vanished, but I could still feel the paradoxically airy yet hefty feel of the blade. I gave her an experimental swing, and a small shimmer in the air gave away her location. It looked like the air that rose off Austin asphalt in the dead of summer.

"Wow. So, you're alive, huh? Are you possessed by the soul of some long-dead and romantically tragic figure?" I could just imagine it...I cocked my head. "Did you hear that, Wembley? I think my sword just blew a raspberry."

"No surprise there. Possessed by a human...where do you get this stuff? She's not cursed; she's alive."

"Oh, sorry about that." I petted the scrollwork near the hilt apologetically. "I'm new. To vampires, magic, and everything."

But Tangwystl was silent.

"She's a sword of few words. Where am I supposed to keep her?"

"In her scabbard, close. What do I know? I haven't carried one in years, and never a living sword. You'll have to figure that part out."

I had a sneaking suspicion I'd just been had. "Why haven't you ever carried a living sword?"

"Apart from the fact that I've been toting her from house to house for...a long time, they're not actually that common. And Tangwystl doesn't like men."

A small chirping noise came from the vicinity of Tangwystl.

"Did you hear that?" I looked at my new sword.

"Oh yes—even I heard that one." He paused and looked at Tangwystl. "I didn't know she could make actual sounds —something beyond mind-speaking. And I apologize. She doesn't like *working* with men. Won't adopt one as a partner, so even if I'd been interested, she wasn't."

I looked at him. He didn't seem to be fibbing, but I still smelled a suspicious odor of deceit. But...a magic sword! I wanted to jump up and down and do a little dance. I had a magic sword!

"Better put it up before you have a small stroke." Wembley handed me the scabbard.

I slid her into the protective casing, expecting some sign of protest. But she gave a happy sigh of pleasure. Actually, it sounded a lot like me when I put my favorite slippers on. I slung the scabbard over my shoulder.

Wembley readjusted the case and flipped it around to my back. "Works better in modern society, and easier for her to cloak because it follows the line and movement of your body. But you'll have to sort out the details of using a sword in modern society on your own time. I haven't the stamina for it any longer."

No aversion to guns, but Wembley did seem completely uninterested in the concept of swordplay. I'd have to quiz him on the hang-up sometime when I wasn't already stretching hospitality to the limits.

"I do remember that Alex carried his in a similar way. And his is the only magic sword I've seen so far. Although I guess I wouldn't really see them—with cloaking and all that? And I'm pretty sure he didn't talk to his." I thought back to the moment I'd seen his sword at the office. Did he always carry it, and it was simply invisible? But I was pretty certain he hadn't spoken to it.

"He uses a minor illusion to mask his sword—same for any other weaponry he happens to stash on his body. And his is definitely not alive." Wembley chuckled as if the thought was vastly entertaining. Once he'd recovered from his fit of humor, he said, "I think he has some more complex enchantments working on his blade—but again, ask him."

Ask someone else. It seemed to be the Society's motto. And it was vastly annoying. But I wasn't getting anything else out of Wembley. He was in house-flipper mode now.

I followed behind him as he led the way to a room on the opposite side of the house. "The guest bathroom is in the hallway." He flicked on the light. "It's clean—but this one hasn't been through the remodel yet. The contractors just finished the master bath and haven't made it to this one."

It was like a 1970s flashback. Gold, sparkly swirls in the Formica countertops, fixtures straight out of an acid trip, and paneling.

"Paneling in the bathroom?"

"It was a moment in time. But call it beadboard, and suddenly it's modern."

"Oh, yeah. But this isn't that." I could feel my nose wrinkling up. "Really not. What are you doing with the walls?"

"I'm not sure. The accountant me says paint it white and go for a French country home look—but that may not fit with the rest of the house, depending on which direction we go with the kitchen."

"Says interior designer you."

"Bingo." He flipped the light off. "This way to your bedroom. Breakfast at eight? Or nine? How about you help yourself if I'm not up?"

"Deal. And thanks for everything, Wembley. I'm sure Alex is being overcautious."

Wembley hesitated and then nodded. "Good night."

The room was cute and fresh. Light bamboo flooring, off-white walls, and sage window panels. There was a unique built-in dresser that I'd never seen in a ranch-style house of this era. Probably added by one of the former owners, Wembley left it mostly as is, only adding a coat of fresh paint and some new handles. I set Tangwystl gently on top of it.

After a quick bathroom trip to freshen up, I changed into my nightgown and slipped into bed. As the sheets slid softly against my skin, I realized this was the first time I'd gone to bed and fallen asleep in any normal fashion since my transformation. There was something comforting about the nightly ritual of brushing teeth, changing into nightclothes, and going to bed. Even in a strange house and a strange bed.

Whoever came to view the house would see in this room exactly what they needed: a spare room for guests, the new baby's room, a home office for freelance work—the possibilities were numerous. I saw safety, routine, and normalcy. And those were the thoughts I fell asleep to.

19

A GIRL AND HER SWORD ARE NEVER PARTED

I jerked in my sleep and woke in a heart-thudding rush.

My breath came in gasps as I lay in bed, trying to remember what nasty dream had woken me. Falling? Topless in algebra? Teeth falling out? Cleaning the junior high boys' bathroom?

Pretty blue eyes...bad man

"Tangwystl? Did you wake me up?"

Bad man

"What?" I tried not to sound peeved, but I hadn't gotten any quality, non-coma sleep in a while. It had been glorious —while it lasted.

Rat

In slow increments, the tiny piston of my groggy mind started to chug away, and something clicked, letting me know that rats weren't good. Rats... "Nuts!" A jolt of adrenaline rushed through me, and I hopped out of bed. More quietly, I asked, "Here? Now?"

Yes...I says you

Tangwystl's petulance was hard to miss.

"Yeah, sorry about that," I whispered as I tiptoed to the dresser. "Any chance you can help a girl out?"

A faint glimmer shone from the edge of the scabbard. I'd take that for a yes.

Whether I knew how to use a sword or not, I didn't have anything else. I grabbed the hilt. My mind flitted to the gun in the kitchen. Too far.

I pulled her free.

Soft singing, just like before.

Holding the sword with both hands, I said quietly, "Any helpful hints?"

Pointy end out

I turned to the door and waited—pointy end out.

Several seconds passed with my heart thudding into the silence.

I wanted to shush it. It seemed like a bad idea, combining a loudly thudding heart and a prowling, murderous vamp. Then I remembered Wembley's nugget of vamp wisdom: vamps didn't drink vamp blood. I only wished knowing that helped.

I crept to the door as quietly as I could. Open the door? Investigate? Wait? I waited a few more seconds—which filled with silence.

Maybe Tangwystl was wrong.

The crash of shattering glass filled my ears. Humid, hot air pressed in on me. Stinging bites prickled the backs of my bare arms and legs.

I turned to the window, now shattered. Why hadn't I thought about the window? I sucked at this.

"You do."

"Ack!" He was inside. Inside the house. Inside my head. Ick. Ick-ick-ick. My flesh crawled.

A sharp nip at my shoulder cleared my head. The rat

had bitten me. My sword tip rested uselessly on the ground, forgotten. I lifted Tangwystl and swung wildly.

By the time my spinning head told me I'd done more than a full circle or three, I realized the rat had retreated. Or was invisible...and insubstantial?

Or the spinning room was confusing me.

"Ow!"

Another sharp nip; this time my other shoulder.

"Tangwystl? Any helpful hints?" This time I tried to move the blade more than my body. If I fell on the ground from lightheadedness—all bad.

"How cute—a magic sword. But if you don't know how to use it..."

Pain spiked as he sliced through the flesh on the back of my arm.

How? And where was Wembley? And why didn't I have a gun? And why me?

"You're pathetically whiny as a vamp. You're almost as bad as you were before. And don't be confused; you were an insufferably entitled bitch before."

I gasped. "You did not. And I wasn't." I didn't think I was.

He laughed. "And that gun you're so interested in? Not very helpful against my kind."

"You...you perv. You've been eavesdropping on my thoughts. My personal, private thoughts."

I shot a few choice images his way.

He just laughed.

I twirled myself to the light switch near the door, the blade tip circling the air around me. I hated to do it—but I had to do it. I couldn't fight what I couldn't see.

I flicked the lights on. Just like I thought, I was blinded for a split second.

"Oooooh, you little rat."

His attack had shredded my nightgown—my only night-gown—and dug a thin furrow in my back.

He had to be slashing with his fangs. Harder to get purchase on my back versus the fleshy part of my arm.

"I'm no rodent."

I scanned the room. I was looking for that hazy, shimmering air that had given away Tangwystl. "Well, when you scurry around in the shadows, fearful of the light of day, you can see how I'd come to that conclusion."

And there it was, not a shimmer; I caught a hint of blurred colors—movement. I lifted the tip of the blade and slashed. "Nuts!"

"I'm too fast for you, little baby vamp." His voice placed him near the bed, but without movement, I couldn't track him.

"Don't suppose that's what you meant by your kind and guns?"

He laughed. "This is fun. More fun than the humans."

The humans. Mrs. A, Liz, my long-disappeared human self. Those three other woman—maybe more—who'd died secret, hidden deaths. I didn't need Tangwystl to tell me my eyes weren't pretty blue any more.

"I will end you." And I believed I might. My vision had sharpened, and all of my senses vibrated like the very best of caffeine-sugar highs. I was ready.

"Will you?" He sounded amused. "Live a few decades, sweetie. Or a few centuries, and then maybe. Oh, how sad. You won't make it that long."

This time, I not only saw the blurred motion, but I traced it as the rat charged me. I slashed. A guttural noise escaped my throat. No hit.

So close. I'd missed—but so had he. I could feel the rub

of my tiny fangs against my lower lip, and I might be snarling.

Too late

I practically spat in frustration. "I *know* that."

Pointy edge out

"I got that part." I wiggled the tip of the blade. "See?"

Guess rat's bite...pointy edge out. A string of unintelligible words poured forth, followed by a groan of frustration. *Predict?*

And while I chatted with my less-than-helpful magical sword—"Owwweeee!"—the rat took a nice, piercing stab at my leg.

Panting, I yelled, "I am going to slice your balls off!"

Tears threatened—just what I needed. Bloody extremities and an acid bath. But then it clicked. Limited language skills, yes, but it was there. "Tangwystl, you angel."

The rat snorted. "You're so incredibly stupid. Tangwystl? What sword calls itself the broker of peace?"

My vamp-enhanced red-eye vision saw him approach. A little geometry, a small sidestep, and the rat impaled himself on my beautiful blade.

"Ha! Gotcha!"

And there he was, fully visible, on the end of my clever blade.

Pin to the wall! Stabby, stabby fast.

"Oh—right!" I scrambled and started to shove him toward the wall. Because who knew how fast he'd be, even with a huge hole in his side?

And that was when I realized that he was the bartender from the bar on Tuesday night. And even if he did wear skinny jeans, he was a lot bigger than me. And he was trying to un-impale himself.

"Nuts!" I shoved the blade as hard as I could—could feel

it sink in another crunchy inch—but he was definitely stronger than me.

"Tangwystl," I panted. "Might have a problem." My bare feet started to slide on the bamboo flooring.

The bedroom door swung open.

Turn to see and maybe lose my footing...don't turn and maybe Wembley accidentally-on-purpose shoots me. Hm.

"And here I thought you might need saving."

Alex.

I almost crumpled in relief. With Alex and Wembley—surely Wembley was here somewhere—and me, we should be able to restrain one homicidal maniac.

"I'm not a homicidal maniac. You're an insect with an inflated ego."

"Aaaaaaaah!" Tangwystl slid another inch. "Stop reading my mind, you pervy...ugh...sicko...ugh...nut job!"

A hysterical giggle burbled. That must have been a few more inches.

As I was not so slowly losing my marbles and grunting my way to several more inches of gut-slicing damage, Alex walked behind the rat, slipped a cord around his neck, and had his ankles trussed to his throat in seconds.

"You can stop now." Alex was definitely trying not to laugh. "And vamps don't get breathless. I believe that's what they call a psychosomatic response."

Having someone tell you not to be out of breath—shockingly—doesn't make you not out of breath. I let go of Tangwystl and backed away until I hit the wall. Then I leaned against it and slid down to the ground. Panting, I said, "Do we also not get sore muscles? Because liar, liar, pants on fire." I rubbed my neck. "I hurt."

Alex sobered. "I'm sorry. Maybe a warm bath?" He yanked my sword out of Bart the bartender.

"Can you guys get all lovey-dovey later? You're going to make me puke."

"Is it just me, or does this nutter seem very not concerned about being captured?" I accepted the bloodied sword with my left hand. The right didn't want to move.

"It's the new order, baby vamp." Black eyes stared into mine. His pupils were huge, with only tiny rings of pale grey iris. "Stayed under the radar; you can't touch me."

You'd think I'd be mad. Or burst into acid tears. Or simply twist the sword in his gut—since leaving it sticking in his midsection alone wasn't causing him a lot of pain. No —I laughed.

And I laughed some more. My sides started to cramp, and I did eventually tear up. But what were a few poisonous tears shed? Because this was reminding me of a certain conversation in a certain office in a certain Society's head-quarters.

I dabbed at my eyes with my nightgown. "You idiot. You're going to hang."

"No way." He looked genuinely confused. He'd killed who knew how many women—because we were insects with inflated egos? What did that even mean? But having committed those crimes, he truly believed he would not be punished.

"Can we just hang him here? Maybe in the backyard?" I asked.

Alex seemed to consider my words. "Eh, better not. Like he said, there is a new order. We'll take Bart—Bart Kegler? —back to Society headquarters for that."

"I don't understand." Bart looked dazed.

I'd thrown around the crazy tag a lot, but now he looked bewildered, like a five-year-old who knows he's broken the rules but simply can't comprehend that he's being punished.

"You forgot about me." I gave him a hard look. Those other women—the ones he'd tried to diminish with his small words—they'd get their justice through me. "I am *not* under the radar. I am very much a loud and visible error."

"But...you're basically an unapproved transformation."

Alex shook his head. "The second unapproved transformation to appear in a human doctor's office. The first went into full bloodlust at the office and seriously injured a nurse. Three unapproved transformations. Three very public incidents."

"I'm also super broken, in case you haven't heard. Can't eat blood, stunted fangs. Also your fault, as my progenitor. My existence makes certain members of the Society very uncomfortable." I shrugged. "Or so I hear."

Was I acting as judge and jury? Oh yes. And I didn't feel the faintest flutter of remorse.

This was about justice. For so many people's lives, both ended and damaged. This underground Society I'd joined, with its odd bureaucracy and funny traditions, its twisty rules and strange members, was my new world. And they said let him hang. I could do that.

20

ONE OF THESE IS NOT LIKE THE OTHERS

Turned out, Wembley had disappeared for reinforcements. And who did he reappear with? My favorite enhanced being, Mr. Clean, a.k.a. Anton the Silent.

We all piled into Anton's black Escalade, complete with a security company logo on the door. I figured Anton for a bouncer—but upscale security guard worked, too.

"Are we at all worried that he's back there tied up with bits of paracord?"

"Bewitched paracord," Alex said. "And it's only a few miles."

The group lapsed into silence.

What seemed like seconds later, Alex was shaking my shoulder. "Wake up."

I'd fallen asleep in just the few miles between Wembley's place and the Society's headquarters—I had to be exhausted. Whatever Alex said about what vamps could and could not do, I'd worn myself out wrestling with Bart the bartender. After having met him, and now that we were marching him to a well-earned death, the appellation "rat" seemed wildly inappropriate. He was both so much more and so much less.

Anton retrieved Bart from the rear of the Escalade, but as I moved to follow them inside, Alex stopped me.

"Wembley, you, and I are going to give testimony, and then we're done. As an injured party, you're invited to stay for the execution—but I wouldn't recommend it."

"I get it now, why people don't like vamps." My lip curled. "It's the God complex."

"Hey," Wembley said with a hurt look. "I don't have a God complex."

Alex punched Wembley in the arm—hard. "You couldn't. You'd have to choose a god."

"True." Wembley smiled good-naturedly, which made me wonder exactly how many gods he worshiped. Turning to me, he said, "Bart might have been of a particularly nasty variety of vamp due to his peculiar type of enhancement. Telepathic vamps always go wrong in the end."

Great. Bart was basically my vamp dad. "Enhancements aren't inherited through progenitors, are they?"

"Not at all. Genetics or a roll of the dice." Wembley put his arm around my shoulders, and we headed inside. I didn't comment, but Wembley was definitely propping me up. I was crashing hard.

Alex opened the door for us—so maybe it was obvious.

"Anyone want to tell me what we're doing exactly? You said we're giving testimony."

"Just a briefing." Alex sped up a bit to open the next door for us.

Yep. I must look pretty rough. "Oh! Any chance for some coffee?" Even the thought perked me up. We'd just left the retail store, and I stopped outside of Alex's office door. "Please?"

Alex hovered, undecided.

"Bad idea." Wembley had removed his arm when I'd stopped. He reached out now and placed his hand in between my shoulder blades.

I hadn't even realized I'd been swaying until he steadied me. "See? I need it."

And now I sounded like a druggie desperate for a fix. Caffeine *was* a drug. I shook my head. A tiny pick-me-up, hardly the same thing.

Alex sighed. "Fine. I have some instant for emergencies."

I vaguely remembered batting my eyelashes for a second cup and reminding Alex of my awesome tolerance —three whole French presses before I'd even noticed the effects—to finagle a third cup. But he and Wembley absolutely cut me off after three, much as I begged for a fourth.

I was feeling positively lively by the time we made it back to the hallway. Everything was fantastic...up until the ghouly ghosty thing.

I squinted at Alex, cocked my head, and leaned close— but no matter what I did, the little ghosty thing was still there, clinging to his back.

Alex frowned at me. "What is it?"

"Um, you remember Great-Auntie Lula?" Alex gave me a brusque nod. "Well, it's just..." I sighed. "Wembley? Can you give us a second?" I tapped him on the nose with my index finger.

Wembley closed his eyes and shook his head. "Clearly you can't hold your coffee quite as well when you're tired. All right. But hurry up."

After he'd disappeared down the hall, I leaned close to Alex and whispered loudly, "There's a ghosty thing hanging on to your back."

A muscle leapt in his jaw and he scanned the hallway then turned hard eyes on me. "I know. But how do you?"

I blinked then shrugged. Maybe I shouldn't have had that third cup. I really didn't understand what was going on.

Alex ran his hands through his hair. "It's just because I'm tired. They sense weakness. But, Mallory, you can't say anything."

I nodded. "Sure thing, chief."

"I'm serious. It would be bad for me, but really, really bad for you." He rubbed his eyes with his thumb and fore-finger. "I'll explain it to you tomorrow when you're sober. But not a word tonight, okay?"

I stood up straight. "Absolutely. I can do that."

And I lived up to my promise. We gave Cornelius a brief-ing, just as Alex had said: found the bad guy, bad guy broke in, captured bad guy—done.

And that was the testimony. Cornelius even cut me a check on the spot—once Alex had reminded him.

That was most of the tale, except... "How did Bart find me squirreled away at Wembley's house?" I'd waited until we left Cornelius in his office. And I tried not to think where Anton and Bart likely were.

Wembley huffed. "And how did Alex get there so fast? I was passed out in the living room, so *I* didn't call him." He looked embarrassed. "He surprised me. Must have been in a hurry, otherwise he'd have done more damage to me."

Alex turned to Wembley. "You have got to start training again. I had no idea you'd gotten so—"

"Complacent? Unaware? Unfit? I think my sabbatical has gone on a few centuries too long." Wembley pinched the bridge of his nose. "Training at noon tomorrow?"

Alex clapped a hand on his back. "Done."

"Okay—I'm really glad you guys have a workout plan set

up, but if Wembley didn't call you, how did you know to come to the house?" I let the "centuries" comment slide, but mostly because my brain simply couldn't grasp the concept that Wembley was that old. Not in its current state.

"The hottie—ah, the blonde bartender from the bar called to see if I wanted to grab a beer after her shift." Alex paused and gave me a curious look.

That was when I realized I was making a funny growling noise. I stopped and frowned. "What? I'm not allowed to be fake pissed that my fake boyfriend was getting hit on?"

"I won't be so easily persuaded the next time you want a coffee hit," Alex said. "But the whole point is that she mentioned Bart had come to work after Joe injured himself moving some boxes, and he claimed to have found your lost keys. She wanted to know if he'd called yet."

"Huh, but there weren't any... Ooooh." I wrapped my tired but caffeinated brain around that thought. "But how did Bart get from 'they're onto me' to 'Mallory's at Wembley's house'?"

"The bartender, I'm sure," Alex said.

I suppose we'd chatted about our plans; they'd hardly been top secret. But I didn't specifically remember that. "And even if she didn't think any of our conversation worth mentioning, all she had to do was have a stray thought, because Bart is telepathic."

"Exactly." We'd reached Alex's office. He motioned to the door. "It's late, and I need to get some rest."

I tried not to blink at the mention of rest, but it reminded me of the spirit creature that had clung to Alex's back earlier. At some point, it had quietly disappeared. Interesting and odd. What had chased him away? Lack of success, I hoped.

I glanced at Wembley. "How are we getting home?"

"I've got it covered."

He seemed sure, so I waved a goodnight to Alex and followed Wembley out to the parking lot.

A few seconds later, I stopped and gave Wembley the are-you-nuts look. "Anton's Escalade?"

Wembley reached under the rear passenger wheel well and pulled out a hide-a-key triumphantly. "Absolutely."

I didn't mention that Anton was an enforcer. Or that he seemed to work for—maybe owned—a security company, that maybe this wasn't a good idea. Because I just wanted to go home and get some rest.

The funny thing? Not once in thinking of home did I think of my condo. As I went to bed for the second time that night, this time on Wembley's sofa, I felt comfortable. I felt like I was at home.

I didn't give Bart more than a passing thought—he didn't deserve any more of my time. I did think about Mrs. A and Liz. I also thought about the other victims.

And right before I fell asleep, I thought about a tiny spirit clinging to Alex's back, whispering in his ear.

Two shakes later, a bright light shone directly in my eyes.

"Wake up." Alex sat on the edge of the sofa backlit by sunlight.

"It's a lie." I pulled the pillow he'd removed back over my head.

"What's a lie?"

"The sun." My words were muffled by the pillow, but I didn't care. The world was too bright. "I've only been asleep a few hours."

"Try ten; it's noon." He tugged on the pillow, but I held it firmly in place. "I have carrot juice."

"Really?"

"Promise. Besides, we need to talk before Wembley and his crew get back. They've made a supply run to fix the bedroom window." His weight left the sofa.

I groaned. Then I remembered fragments of a rather unpleasant dream I'd had. I pulled the pillow off my head, ready to be blinded, but Alex had pulled the curtains. I sighed in relief. "Thanks. I had a rather unpleasant dream that involved you. I think it was you." Shaking my head, I said, "Who knows? Dreams are weird. Bart?"

He sat down in an armchair a few feet away. "Executed last night."

"Whoa—they don't mess around. Good thing he was actually guilty." I made a mental note not to ever be falsely accused—oh, right, I couldn't control that.

"Expedited execution due to a confession of the accused. Truth extraction is rather...unpleasant, so he confessed to avoid the ordeal."

I remembered that odd comment about the Inquisition and shivered. The Society might talk a big game about bringing in a new order... "Torture is notoriously unreliable. You guys know that, right?"

"Possibly, but we have a witch come in to verify all confessions."

"This conversation is making me feel icky. I know we did the right thing by turning him over, but the Society is looking pretty shady. And don't say it; I already know: you're all working toward a better solution." I sat cross-legged on the sofa and pulled the blanket up high under my chin. All of this talk about torture reminded me of a question I'd been meaning to ask for a while now. "Quick question about your sword."

Alex pulled out his phone and checked the time. "Go ahead."

"Does your sword talk to you?"

"My sword doesn't speak to me, because mine isn't actually alive. It's imbued with magical incantations and the substance itself is an alchemic alloy—but it is most certainly not alive. Living things have will. They make choices. I don't want my sword—a tool intended to serve my will—to make decisions."

"Oh. Oops. Did Wembley pull a fast one on me?"

"Yeah, oops. I can't believe he thought giving you Tangwystl was a good idea."

"I could lock her up..." But the idea held no appeal. She'd been locked away for so long already, waiting for the right person. And she'd chosen me.

Alex sighed. "But you don't want to, because you like her. That's one of the other problems with living objects: you get attached. They have opinions and make choices, and you start to treat them like people. Tangwystl isn't a person trapped in a sword—she's a living sword. Don't forget that."

"Does that mean you think I should keep her?"

"A living sword isn't my own choice for a sword, but I suspect you wouldn't have fared so well in the confrontation with Bart without her."

His comments were translating into a stamp of approval in my mind, so I was glad I asked. I liked Tangwystl. Sure, her vocabulary was seriously limited, but at least she spoke English. That seemed pretty cool, given how old she was.

"Also—this whole carrying a sword in public thing," I said. "How does that work?"

"You'll have to sort that out with her. Mine has incantations inscribed to conceal and store it."

Store it...I remembered him driving in the car with no obvious sword. Sitting at my office desk with no sword. "Are you telling me your sword gets stashed somewhere until you need it?"

"Basically. And when it is present, most can't see it. Better to ask Tangwystl your sword questions. I have no idea what she's capable of." He glanced at his cell phone. "You had a question about some dream? If you hadn't taken forever to wake up, we'd have more time." He gave me a narrow-eyed look. "Too much coffee."

"I do feel a little hungover." Which reminded me—I grabbed the carrot juice bottle from the coffee table and gulped down several swigs. "So this guy in my dream—maybe you, maybe not you—has no face. And he has these strings attached, like a marionette, but different because all the strings are to the guy's chest—or maybe his torso? Which is weird, because marionettes have little strings all over, otherwise you can't move all the pieces."

"So if he has no face, why is he me?"

I finished the juice and wiped my mouth with the back of my hand. "I don't know." I peered intently at him. "But since you seem to think he is, too, why don't you tell me?"

Alex leaned back in the armchair and propped his foot on his knee. "About what you saw last night—"

"The spirit."

"The caffeine-induced hallucination." He looked at me.

"Are you kidding me? I know what I saw, drunk on coffee or not."

"This isn't about me." He rubbed his eyes with thumb and forefinger. "It's not only about me. Vamps don't see spirits."

"Whatever. Vamps also survive by drinking blood, have great big serpenty fangs, and don't get out of breath or cry acid tears. Newsflash: that garbage isn't right."

He looked nonplussed. "Acid tears?"

"Oh, yeah. I could totally bottle that stuff and sell it. Weaponized tears."

Alex rolled his head back and groaned. "Keep that one to yourself if you can. But the spirits, you cannot tell anyone else. Communicating with spirit entities is a wizard power. Vamps don't see spirits, can't communicate with spirits." He gave me a fierce, angry look. "Can't control spirits. And if certain people were to think otherwise, that could cause a lot of problems for you."

"And what about you and that thing clinging to you?"

"Gone. I just needed a little sleep."

The futon in his office, the healthy food in his fridge, leaving half a glass of perfectly good scotch... "Good grief. You probably don't smoke, jog every day, and take vitamins."

"If it keeps them off my back—literally—that's right."

"Wild guess: not all wizards have this particular issue." I flashed back to the image from yesterday. That thing was definitely whispering in Alex's ear.

"No."

I crooked my pinky and offered it. "Pinky swear?"

"You're kidding."

"Since the only secret I've ever pinky sworn on is still safe twenty years after the fact, no, I'm not kidding."

He squeezed his eyes shut with a pained look. But when he opened them, he hooked his pinky with mine.

I nodded grimly. "Pinky swear, I won't tell yours, if you don't tell mine."

Alex sighed. "Pinky swear."

Little blue-green sparks flew as soon as Alex said "swear."

I yanked my hand back. "Whoa—what did you do?"

"Not me."

The front door opened. Wembley was home.

21

BAREFOOT HERO

"We've got a window patch." Wembley made the announcement as he came through the front door. When no one applauded, he sighed. "Well, I was excited about it."

I stood up, stretched, and headed for the kitchen. "I don't suppose either of you know what I did with that check last night?"

Alex and Wembley followed me. Alex pulled out his wallet and extracted a check. Handing it to me, he said, "Since you weren't quite yourself last night."

"Very appreciated."

Wembley sat down at the breakfast table. "I've already eaten—you're welcome—but I can keep you company while you empty my fridge of all consumable liquids."

"Minus milk and eggs," I said with a moue of distaste, looking at the contents of the fridge. "And I used to like eggnog so much."

"And no steak," Wembley said.

Alex peered over my shoulder. "Since when is steak a liquid?"

"Since Wembley's amazing food processor can liquefy it."

"Why...? No. Just no." Alex pulled a small bottle of kefir out of the fridge. "Since you can't drink it. Thanks."

I hunted till I found the carton of carrot juice and started to chug it. About a quarter of the way through, I thought about taking a breath, then chugged another quarter. I took a gasping breath and asked, "What exactly is a window patch? Sounds kinda fancy."

"Hm. Plywood," Wembley said. "The guys are installing it now."

In the background, I could hear the rhythmic thud of hammers. I'd just been tuning it out.

A ringtone that might have been my mother's special, preprogrammed tone jingled in the background.

"Ugh. That's got to be mine. Any clues where my cell landed? My mother probably thinks I'm dead."

Wembley handed my phone to me, mouthing something.

I held my finger up. "Hi, Mother." Then I pointed to the back door, and Wembley nodded.

"Sorry. I just have to run outside."

"Outside—why are you not at work?"

I'd forgotten—she had no idea I'd quit my job. I looked up at the brilliantly blue sky. Too bad I wasn't religious, because now would be the perfect moment to pray to God for patience.

"So, Mother, a little change...I've given notice at work."

"Given notice—you quit?" She sounded befuddled more than upset.

Maybe it wouldn't be so bad...

"You lose your job—"

"I quit. That's not losing a job; that's walking away." I sat down in one of Wembley's incredibly comfortable lawn chairs. Why had the guys mentioned steak? Now I was dying for a cheeseburger. Except not really, because I would just puke it right back up. My stomach lingered on the memory of meat even though the reality made it unhappy—it was a weird feeling. And I guessed that aversion therapy hadn't helped for very long after all.

"And what about your beautiful apartment? Did you quit it, too? Mrs. Franklin lives in your building. She heard you were moving out."

"Did Mrs. Franklin mention anything else?" I squinted up at the tree shading the yard. But for the potential for bird droppings, a perfectly shady spot for some more lawn furniture.

"No. Should she have?"

"No, not at all," I replied, trying to hide my relief. I crossed my fingers. "I think I might have found a new place in southeast Austin." I'd be having a look at Wembley's other place soon, I was sure. And I had a good feeling about it.

But I couldn't help but be glad I'd dodged explaining anything to do with Mrs. A's death. The official story had shifted but was still unpalatable. No longer an accidental overdose or suicide, now there were rumors of a suspicious death. I doubted someone had realized Mrs. A would never kill herself or do anything by accident, so the police must have found some evidence of foul play. Good luck finding the killer, coppers. At least I knew the truth. Nuts. Bradley. I'd have to text him; seemed better than calling—

My mom raised her voice. "Are you even listening?"

Oops. I'd kinda tuned her out there for a bit. "Sorry, what were you saying?"

Mother let out an exasperated sigh. "The job, the apartment, the car... Sweetheart, are you sure you're all right?"

I sat up straighter. Was I all right? Only a few weeks ago, I'd never have made the huge, life-altering choices I was making now. But I was happy.

"What would you say if I told you I'd never felt like this before? I think I'm really happy." My stomach cramped. Starving, yes—but I'd nabbed a killer. My life was in complete chaos, sure—and yet I *was* happy. "I have to go, Mother. I need to grab a snack before my stomach eats itself —but I promise you, I really am okay."

Mom sniffed. Was she crying?

"That's all I ever wanted for you, sweetheart. But the suburbs..." My mother's voice firmed. "But if the suburbs make you happy, then you go live in the suburbs."

I didn't have the heart to tell Mom that southeast Austin wasn't exactly the suburbs. Not when she was trying so hard to accept the new and strange woman I'd become. Besides, anything outside the heart of downtown probably was the 'burbs as far as Mom was concerned.

"Thanks, Mother."

"Oh, and tell your friend I look forward to seeing him tomorrow. Bye-bye now." And she hung up.

My friend? I stared at the phone.

Wembley.

I headed back inside, wavering between amused and terrified.

"Wembley?"

"Don't look," Wembley called from the kitchen. "Hide your eyes. Just having a quick snack."

My nose picked up on the smell before he'd said "snack."

"Right—I can smell it." I pinched my nose. At least I

wasn't about to ralph. That was an improvement. "My mother, Wembley?"

"Ah. I did try to mention it. I answered your phone earlier this morning. When you were still passed out from your coffee hangover. She called twice. Any mother who calls twice...well, it was that or wake you up." Water ran in the sink, and then he called out, "All clear."

I unplugged my nose and sniffed cautiously. Barely any odor at all. I joined him in the kitchen. "How do you go from answering my phone to attending a luncheon as her date?" Because their little "date" had to be that luncheon she'd invited me to last week. "Any thoughts about the whole eating solids thing?"

"No problem."

I rolled my eyes. My mother and Wembley hanging out was definitely a problem waiting to happen. "Where's Alex?"

"He's on call today. Lemann brought him in to deal with another potential Bart victim."

"What? Without me?" A nasty thought occurred. "Ugh. He's not the axman, is he?"

Wembley shrugged. "I didn't ask for details."

"So not good." I pulled up Alex's number. Tucking the phone under my chin, I asked Wembley, "Where's my bag? I need to change—pronto."

He nodded and disappeared.

Alex picked up on the first ring. "I was just about to call you."

"Uh-huh. Sure you were." I nodded my thanks to Wembley as he handed me my bag. "Where are you?" I made a circle with my finger, and Wembley turned his back.

"I'm over at headquarters."

I pulled off my nightgown. "Got it. There in five."

"Wait—"

I hung up before he could tell me not to come. Who knew what state that poor woman was in? And the Society, with their Inquisition and their lickety-split executions —not good.

I yanked on clothes as fast as I could. Once decently clothed, I said, "I'm good, Wembley. You can turn around. Where are my keys?"

He handed them to me.

I kissed his cheek. "You're a doll. I'll call with an update."

"Shoes?"

Nuts. I'd just about left barefoot. I hunted around for my All Stars and finally found them under the couch. Socks were a lost cause. I tucked them under my arm and hotfooted it to the front door.

"Wait!" Wembley called from the kitchen.

"In a rush—"

"I know, I know." Wembley appeared, a bottle of spicy vegetable juice in hand.

"Ha! Perfect." I grabbed the bottle. "Toodles."

I drove to headquarters barefoot, chugging my tangy-awesome juice the whole way. Something about the spicy-salty combo made it a little more satisfying than other drinks. I probably needed to pursue the salt angle a little deeper.

I zipped into the Society's parking lot and parked next to Alex's black Honda.

As I weighed faster and barefoot against the need for footwear, I heard a woman scream, "Noooooo!"

Decision made, I tucked my shoes back under my arm and flat-out ran to the front door. When I arrived, the front door was locked—I needed a dang key for this place.

I thudded the tinted glass door with my open palm. When that didn't work, I made a fist and thumped harder.

"Coming." Alex's voice had an edge to it.

He opened the front door with a look of relief. "Thank God. Get in here." He yanked me inside by my forearm and locked the door behind me. "I've already sent the staff home, but this...this I cannot handle."

And then I heard it—a woman saying, "No, no, no, no."

Alex propelled me further into the store and then pointed two aisles ahead. "Whatever you can do..."

He ran a hand through his hair.

I tiptoed toward the aisle in question, unsure what horror had stumped Alex, former knight and enforcer and on-call emergency responder.

Nuts. I'd forgotten Tangwystl. I was pretty sure I'd left her in Wembley's spare room...

I turned the corner of the aisle.

22

LIFE SUCKS? GET A LIFE COACH

A terry cloth robe and bunny slippers.

That was what I noticed first. Next came the flame-haired woman wearing them. And then—hard to believe this wasn't the first thing I registered—the gooey red-colored corn syrup that covered her.

She was huddled on the floor directly in front of the fake blood display.

Very real fangs protruded from her mouth. Not so small as mine, but smaller than Wembley's. Not a baby vamp— maybe just a hungry one?

In a disappointed, the-world-had-just-crumbled-under-her-feet voice, she said, "It's just syrup."

I sighed. Probably very hungry.

My phone beeped with a text from Alex: *Hates men.*

Aha.

"Would you like some blood?"

With sad puppy-dog eyes, she blinked and nodded.

"All right, then, let's get you some, shall we?"

She perked up, and her fangs extended further. Yikes. About the same as Wembley's, but I'd never seen the actual descent or retraction happen. They just seemed to be there —or not. Moving fangs were super freaky.

I smiled. It was harder to look scared when you smiled. And those fangs were creeping me out.

"I don't haaf to bite anything?" She certainly managed to speak with those monster serpent fangs better than I could.

"No. No biting. There's a fridge out back."

She melted in relief. And what she meant by biting "anything," I didn't really want to know. Could vamps survive on non-human blood? Another factoid to pursue that had absolutely nothing to do with my own vampire experience.

I reached a hand out to help her up. "What's your name?"

"Gladys." She leveraged herself to a standing position using my hand for balance.

And it was like a Liz flashback: gorgeous cheekbones, long legs, and all. Except for the clothes. Liz had fabulous taste in clothes.

"How exactly did you get here?"

She angled her head. "My car."

"And you found the Society how?"

She looked at me like I'd gone mad. "The internet?"

Right—why not? Bits, Baubles, and Toadstools definitely had a website.

"Excellent. Well, let's you get you a snack." She blinked sad eyes at me, and I immediately corrected myself. "A very large meal. We'll get you sorted."

I bade a fond farewell to my clothes, and then put an arm around her very red, very sticky shoulders.

We left the aisle for the main area of the store to find Alex patiently waiting to escort us to the blood supply in the back of the warehouse.

She jerked and squealed like a stuck pig.

I hugged her with one arm and waved him away with the other.

The moment he disappeared, she fell silent. My ears might not forgive Alex that little misstep.

"I'll just unlock the door and prop it open, shall I?" His voice carried over the aisle shelving, but was muffled.

I herded Gladys out of sight down another aisle. "All right."

"Go ahead," Alex said.

Arm around her shoulders, I walked Gladys through the "Employees Only" door to the back of the warehouse. I propped her against the hall wall and said, "Stay. Don't move. I'll be right back, I promise."

And then I slipped back into the retail area. "Alex? Where are you?"

He appeared from behind the register. "Hiding." He had the grace to look just a little embarrassed.

"Text me directions to the blood stash." When he raised his eyebrows, I wrinkled my nose at him and said, "I'll be fine. Oh, and clear the hallways. Please."

He snorted. "Done five minutes ago. My ears are still ringing."

"What happened with the salesgirl? She's human, right?"

"Actually, no. But she called when a lady in a house robe, slippers, and nothing else appeared in the store. I sent her for a long lunch and told her to call before she comes back in." Alex ran his hand through his already very rumpled hair. "She remembers some things. I think. It's hard to say— but sedatives can be tricky. I think, unlike you, she knows something about what happened to her."

"Well, that just sucks for her. I'll do what I can to sort her out." A thought occurred. A brilliant thought: I might have found my calling. I grinned at him.

"What? That look cannot be good."

"Just call me the *after*-life coach." I crossed my arms. "The Society will be receiving my bill for services rendered. And tell Cornelius that if he doesn't pay up promptly, I won't help the next time you have a fake-blood-soaked vampire damsel in distress."

A total lie, but I was technically unemployed, and a girl had to get her pennies where she could. And I liked the idea. After-life coaching seemed like something I might take to. I'd been managing my own transition rather fabulously, and had come out smelling like a bouquet of fresh flowers, if I did say so myself.

"I need to get back to Gladys."

"Gladys, huh?" He laughed. "Well, at least you got a name out of her. Work on a last name, if you don't mind."

"Will do." I hustled back to the "Employees Only" door, turning to shoo Alex out of sight before I opened it. Couldn't have my new client melting eardrums or wandering the halls in her bunny slippers.

THE END

THE CLIENT'S CONUNDRUM (VEGAN VAMP #2) PREVIEW

Chapter One: Where's the Bathroom?

The woman at the front of the room smiled in that bland, uninterested way that people do when they'd given a presentation fifteen times too many and couldn't be bothered if you were listening or not.

"I know that some of you are new to the area, and some of you are new to enhanced living."

At least she had a pleasant voice.

"I've provided each of you with a binder. Inside the binder you'll find..."

Or not so pleasant, because it all sounded like blah, blah, blah. This was going to be an ordeal. And to think I'd been looking forward to the Society's official orientation since I found out that an orientation existed.

The thick binder in my hands was printed with the words "Do Not Remove from Society Headquarters." Well, if you're going to give a girl—vamp—a handbook, you better expect her to take it home.

I wasn't sure how I'd lug three pounds of paper products and a massive 1990s binder out unnoticed, but I'd work it out.

Just as the presenter was getting to the good part—the location of the several bathrooms scattered throughout the warehouse facility—someone's phone rang. Shame on them. A lady needed to know where the facilities were located; you never knew when you'd have a makeup emergency or a wardrobe failure. Because as many fluids as I drank these days, I never seemed to actually need to pee. The wonders of magic.

The phone kept ringing. At some point—three rings later? five?—I realized I'd changed my business forwarded calls ringtone...to that same exact ringtone.

I dug through my purse, considered very briefly silencing the call, then answered, "Just one second."

I started to crawl over the feet and purses of those unfortunate enough to be seated in my aisle. The Society had packed us in like sardines, which was silly with only twelve or fifteen attendees. Couldn't they have given us a bigger room? "So sorry," I said to the woman whose foot I'd just trodden on.

I could hear Gladys's voice as she continued to talk. But I could hardly listen to Gladys, crawl over strangers in a tight space, and make my apologies to the injured. Gladys would have to wait.

Finally, I reached the end of the row, and I turned to give the presenter an apology wave only to find her glaring at me. Oopsie. I waved and smiled anyway then stepped out into the hall.

"I'm so sorry, Gladys. It's just that I have to attend—" I closed my eyes and sighed. "Did you say dead? Next to you?

In bed? Calm down. I'm on my way." I ended the call with a sigh.

Lord above, Gladys had turned into a project. She was probably having bad nightmares again. I headed toward the front of the warehouse building, to the retail shop. It was the easiest exit to the parking lot, and the stock in the store was always entertaining.

I'd helped her through a rough few days when she'd first transitioned. Like me, she'd been bitten and accidentally turned into a vampire. Our progenitor—a nasty creature who'd hanged for his crimes—had been gorging on the blood of women he found particularly annoying. In the midst of that, he'd killed several women (not a Society crime) and turned loose a few baby vamps on the world— and we'd been too noticeable in our untrained dismay (definitely a Society crime).

I had no memory of my particular neck-biting trauma, but Gladys remembered small pieces. And since then, men made her very uncomfortable. We'd been working on it. As her undead life coach, it was my job. Gladys was my first client, but we were making great progress.

My cell pinged with a new text message. As I slid my finger across the screen, a photo popped up. I flipped my phone to enlarge the picture...yes, definitely a corpse. Definitely in a bed. Quite possibly Gladys's bed.

As I ran to the front of the building, I couldn't help thinking at least he was a man—we really were making progress if Gladys had been doing the wild with some guy.

But a dead body meant reinforcements were called for. I made a beeline for my favorite investigator-enforcer-knight's office. Dead bodies usually meant all sorts of mess. Political mess, physical mess, maybe even paranormal mess.

Alex was great with messes. And he'd helped me. We shared a sensitive secret, so we were tight.

Knocking lightly produced no result, so I pounded.

"What?" It sounded like Mr. Cranky Pants woke up on the wrong side of the bed.

"It's Mallory." I opened the door to find a half-naked Alex rolling off the futon he used for emergency kip.

A lot of naked chest, but more interesting—that naked chest was covered in tattoos. Symbols, not pictures. And maybe letters? I leaned closer—

"What do you want?" He snatched a T-shirt off the side table and pulled it over his head. I got a glimpse of his shoulders and back, also covered with tats.

And, most interesting of all, the T-shirt he'd thrown on covered every single bit of ink.

"Ah, my client woke up next to a dead body. Any chance you could help a girl out?"

It said a lot about our relationship that he didn't look terribly surprised. "I need fifteen minutes."

"Perfect. You're a complete doll."

He spared me a quick glare before disappearing into the bathroom. The door closed with a loud, firm click.

I did know how important his sleep was to him. That was one half of the secret we shared. The spirits—or demons or elementals; he hadn't really explained the difference—messed with him when he wasn't a hundred percent. As a result, Alex was a bit of a health nut. *How* exactly they messed with him, I didn't know. We hadn't shared quite that much.

Which led to the other half of the secret. Alex hadn't exactly shared that information. I'd seen one of the little nasties clinging to his back in the middle of the night.

Apparently, sleep deprivation wasn't good for staving off the nasty critters.

Alex cracked the door, and I could hear water running. "Who's your client?"

I scrunched up my nose and hoped for the best. "Gladys Pepperman."

His groan was loud enough that I heard it over the running water. I waited—then let out a sigh of relief when he didn't say anything.

Alex poked his head out of the bathroom. "Aren't you supposed to be in orientation?"

I shrugged.

"Did you even go?"

"I went. I can even tell you where all of the bathrooms are."

He stuck his head out again, but this time he was brushing his teeth, so he shot me an exasperated look. "So you pee now?"

"None of your business. A woman—vamp or otherwise —is allowed to retain a little mystery about personal habits."

"That's a no, then?"

I shifted the large orientation binder from one arm to the other. "That's a no. Hey, I don't suppose theft of orientation materials is one of those crimes that leads to swift execution by hanging?"

Something clattered in the bathroom and Alex swore.

"You okay in there?"

"Yes." And not long after, he exited looking brighter-eyed —and wearing a small piece of toilet tissue on his jaw. "You will not be hung for stealing orientation materials. But bring them back. There's some sensitive information inside."

"And no witchy protection spells that do something

nasty—like soak me in dye or make me smell funky—when I cross the headquarters threshold?"

"No, but it's a thought if we keep getting made Society members like you."

Made versus born. Such a bizarre prejudice, but groups would hyper-focus on the differences. Alex was born, naturally.

"Ready?" When he nodded, I chucked my keys at him. He had a thing about driving, so I let him. As the more mature person, it seemed the right thing to do. And Alex's enhanced dexterity and speed meant he had mad driving skills.

"Oh." I pulled up the picture on my phone as he locked his office. "This is the guy."

He glanced at my phone, then closed his eyes. When he opened them, he snatched my phone and examined the picture more closely.

"This is the CEO of the Society."

"No." I knew that guy, and this wasn't that guy. "Cornelius has a beard. And he's shorter, stockier."

"Cornelius is the chief *security* officer. This is the chief *executive* officer."

"Oh." I thought about it. "Uh-oh."

Alex ran his hand through his hair. "Uh-oh is a massive understatement."

§

Want to read more? The Client's Conundrum is now available! http://www.catelawley.com/vegan-vamp-series

BONUS CONTENT

Interested in bonus content for the Vegan Vamp series?
Subscribe to my newsletter to receive a bonus chapter for
Adventures of a Vegan Vamp as well as release
announcements and other goodies! Sign up at
http://eepurl.com/b6pNQP.

ABOUT THE AUTHOR

Cate Lawley is the pen name for Kate Baray's sweet romances and cozy mysteries, including The Goode Witch Matchmaker and Vegan Vamp series. When she's not tapping away at her keyboard or in deep contemplation of her next fanciful writing project, she's sweeping up hairy dust bunnies and watching British mysteries with her pointers and hounds.

Cate also writes urban and paranormal fantasy as Kate Baray and thrillers as K.D. Baray.

For more information:
www.catelawley.com
www.facebook.com/katebaray
www.twitter.com/katebarayauthor

Made in the USA
Monee, IL
17 March 2022